JEF

The First-Person Dilogy

●

Sebastian in a Dream

a novel prompted by and written during the time of the pandemic

●●

The Burial of the Count of Orgaz

a novel prompted by and written during the time of the war

YURIY TARNAWSKY

THE BURIAL OF THE COUNT OF ORGAZ

a novel

2024

Cover Design by Norman Conquest
Author Photo by Ihor Todoruk

ISBN 1-884097-24-3
ISBN-13 978-1-884097-24-9

ISSN 1084-547X

This is volume 101 of
The Journal of Experimental Fiction

JEF Books/Depth Charge Publishing
Arlington Heights, Illinois

JEF Books/Depth Charge Publishing
The Foremost in Innovative Fiction
Experimentalfiction.com

JEF Books and The Journal of Experimental fiction
are distributed to the academic market by EBSCO

To fully perceive the novel, it will be indispensable for the reader to view the El Greco painting, a copy of which is provided at the end of the text. As is the case with its companion, Sebastian in a Dream, *a detailed account of the writing of* The Burial of the Count of Orgaz *can be found in Yuriy Tarnawsky's forthcoming* JEF book *Literary Diary 2020-2024.*

1

TOLEDO, TOLEDO, TOLEDO, the street curves right, no, left, I think, yes, the street curves to the left, and although it looks as though it's blocked, it's walled up, the two walls joined together in a tight corner at the end because all you can see is the left, I mean, the right wall, scarred by vehicles trying to squeeze themselves through the curving, narrow space, it actually isn't because you can see daylight pushing its way into the gray, gloomy, space, the moist cobblestones where it hits them shiny like tram tracks, like street-car tracks, as in the city where father went to school which I visited for the first time many years after he died, many years ago, when I was no longer a young man, a sickening smell of *pommes frites,* no, not of *pommes frites*, of *churros*, the smell of *churros,* and *turrones,* and *mazapanes* in the cold, damp air, as fit, as fit in the case of the last two, for the season, for the time of the year, for Christmas, *So, also hierher kommen die Leute, um zu leben, ich würde eher meinen, es stürbe sich hier, der arme Malte,* why   poor

Yuriy Tarnawsky

Malte? why only him? why only him poor? *andere Leute kommen hierher auch um zu sterben,* nothing tragic, extraordinary in that, it happens every day, here, and there, and everywhere, it happens to everyone, that is, it happens every day to someone, and it happens to everyone one day here, and there, and everywhere, and it so happens that it has happened to me here, I can't see myself from the outside, of course, especially from the back, but I shuffle along like that man in the labor camp, the young Italian guy who was too sick to work and got up only to go to the mess hall three times a day for dishes of hot water of different color and taste, shuffling along, bent over, with a blanket draped over his hunched-up back, actually over his back and head, over his hunched-up back and hung-down head most of the time, for it was cold then, was that time of the year, was the season for it, was winter, around Christmas it must have been, probably around Christmas, the man who died eventually, I think, not sure if because of his health, I mean his lack of health, because of being ill, or because of that air raid, which wrought havoc with the camp and the whole city, churning up everything, time, and space, and buildings, and objects, and people, turning all into a jumble, into rubble, into a huge mess, so, the right wall, scarred by passenger cars of people who live in the neighborhood or of occasional, perhaps lost, visitors, and *camionetas*, delivering goods to the grocery stores in the area, the scratches, scars, deep, deep, painful gashes in the thick grimy, almost black stucco, revealing the bricks underneath, thin, wide, long bricks that look like big, thin, old books, from which most of the city, most of the buildings in the city seem to be built, centuries, many centuries old, but looking new, looking like new, having stood up splendidly to time, to the ravages of time, as new ones, the ones made nowadays, I'm sure, would never, will never do, you can see them also where the walls are pockmarked by bullets, rifle bullets from the civil war, strange that it hasn't been fixed yet after all these years, they probably leave it on purpose, as a memorial to those horrible or glorious times, horrible to those in power now and glorious in the times of Franco, but no, I'm wrong, horrible and glorious to both sides but for different, opposite reasons, in different order, so to speak, you can see them, the marks, the pockmarks all over town like on the walls of the Alcázar, where Moscardó and his intrepid crew holed up for more than two months until they were liberated on September 27,

Yuriy Tarnawsky

1936 by Franco's troops, during those two plus months it was a weekend, Sunday sport, diversion for the *rojos* to take the train or a *camión* from Madrid down to Toledo and do target practice shooting at the structure to get perchance one of the hated *Fascistas,* exchanging bullets and *hijos de puta,* and *hijos de mala madre*, and *me cago en la leche de tu madre, de tu puta madre, que mamaste,* but most visible, visible in particular, the bullet pockmarks, I mean, particularly visible on a building in Plaza de Zocodover, which serves as the *Plaza Mayor*, the Main Square in town, where I sat in a café with her, the second one, drinking, sipping beer, the first time with the second one, and then with the first one, neat, isn't it? ass backwards, what else would you expect from a master, a doctor, a PhD of self-destruction like me, so, where I sat a few, essentially many times with the first one, I bought her, the second one, a bracelet, a beautiful thick *damasquinado*, damascene bracelet, silver and gold on a dull black background, silver maybe silver, but gold, I'm sure, brass, polished brass, the bracelet wasn't that expensive, looked like a plump domesticated snake, the beautiful part of a snake without the slithering, and the open mouth with the two fangs, and the flickering flame-like tongue, so, the bracelet looked like the most beautiful part of a snake, wrapped around her delicate girl's wrist as I put it on for her the morning we were leaving for the south, for Córdoba, Sevilla, Granada, Sevilla, yes, Sevilla and then Granada, not Ronda as with the first one a year or so, no, actually, just a few months later, Córdoba, Sevilla, Granada, Ronda, stopped off with the second one outside the city, on the road circling it, where there is that spot he, El Greco painted the famous *View of Toledo* from, which hangs now in the Prado, nothing like what the city actually looks like, looks like now, but probably never did, didn't in his time, nor before or after, but which it actually is and which he with his X-ray artist's eyes, with his artist's seer eyes that penetrate everything, saw as he saw everything he painted, and which I am seeing every hour of the day, every hour of every day and night, that is, even in my sleep, and which I am seeing now, it's lighter here, airier, not like in the *callejón* I've just stepped out of, a little *plazuela* with the church, a modest, nondescript building at the end, a McDonald's it could almost be, since they are everywhere nowadays and look like anything they want to look, its, the church's bell tower, a square sturdy structure, though, protruding above its roof and above those of a few other buildings up ahead, a Moorish structure by its appearance, I think the church was a *mezquita* and the tower a minaret at the time of the *moros,* built mostly out of those old bricks that look like big old books, which most of the buildings in town seem to be built from, I make a beeline toward it, the church, trace out with my footsteps at a sharp angle a dotted line, a bisectrix across the little square, pass through the door, they let me in without stopping, without asking me to pay, out of goodwill, out of charity, they know me, the *forastero,* the *extranjero,* an Albert Camus and Collin Wilson stranger, the weirdo, who comes every day to stand in front of the painting for a few minutes before leaving, unchanged, there are people in the church, but it remains empty, there's too much daylight, too much daylight is pushing its way in on both sides from above, bringing out, highlighting the emptiness, the fact there's essentially no one there, the two parallel rows of empty benches like signatures of witnesses attesting to the truth, to the emptiness, the chapel on the right, behind the thin black wooden wall of *cuarterones* added for protection, empty too, I mean, really empty, I'm alone, the only one, in it, a large empty bank vault, the cold like six-inch-thick steel plates on all sides, right, left, above below, ahead, behind, straight ahead, behind the low iron railing, on the other side of which the little flower garden of the tomb lies a few feet below the floor level, the painting, a mute, confused, blurred tumult among a few large figures up above, and from a third down, the charcoal-gray, the coaldust-gray of Toledo, the basement, perhaps the boiler room of a large building (the *Ayuntamiento?* the City Hall?*)*, with a low vaulted ceiling, in which a whole bunch of stokers, must be all the members of the town stoker guild, have gathered to witness some unusual, miraculous event taking place, where two human figures that face each other, dressed in voluminous golden robes, are bending down and like two giant hands are lowering, or raising, or simply holding the body of a man who could be dead, or asleep, or simply resting with his eyes closed, no one is moving, stirring, but things are happening, an image, a poetic image of a person appearing in the heart of another one is shaping itself, forming, in the middle, where the man's body sags, fire has started to burn and the charcoal-gray, the coaldust-gray of the armor has begun to turn red, yellow, gold, it sparkles, shines, among the colors, the images of the two leaning figures are coalescing, taking shape, coming into view like fishes, goldfishes, rising up to the surface in the murky waters of a pond in order to be fed, up above, at the moment, only some of the figures, perhaps three or four or five, I don't feel like counting, are looking down, it seems like about as many are looking up, to check what's going on there, and one, I think just one, stares straight ahead, at me, at us, the viewer, while the rest have randomly turned their faces this way and that, mostly toward or away from their neighbor on the left or right, or the other way around, and are staring with unfocused eyes into space, but that's just a coincidence, a moment, the painter's brush has captured as a camera would do nowadays, for we know, the viewer knows that only a brief moment, a mere second, an instant later they all will have turned their heads forward and directed their gaze down at the sagging body, because in each of the figures', of the men's mind there is only one thought, one wish, one desire, to witness the magic moment of a miracle taking place, a lifeless painting on a wall coming alive and turning into a work of art.

2

IT'S A TIGHT space, not small, they say five meters by three, five tall and three wide, but it's packed full with people, well, figures, I mean it's packed full with figures because some of them shouldn't be called people, like angels, that pretty blonde female figure with wings in the middle up above, one or two more ill-defined ones, and a bunch of cherubs, two with bodies and the rest just wings and heads, wings attached to heads, and then this bubble/bauble of a homunculus being pushed up by the winged female figure through the vaginal canal leading up to heaven that's supposed to be the count's soul, I don't know what El Greco had in mind, that the count's soul was just a fetus when inside him and would be born once he died and it entered heavenly space? doesn't make sense, but it's actually wonderful, your death is the birth of your soul, your soul is born when it goes to heaven to sit at Christ's side, while down below it's just something that one day might be if it's not aborted, if it does go to heaven, but maybe El Greco had something else in mind, they didn't know much about anatomy, I mean biology, about being born, in those days, but speaking of anatomy, he appears to have known pretty well what a vaginal canal looks like, most likely from personal amorous experience, at least from that with Jerónima de las Cuevas, the mother of his son Jorge Manuel, his common-law wife, whom he for some reason apparently never married, so he appears to have known what a vaginal, a birth canal looks, that is, feels like through personal amorous experience, mostly his middle finger, I presume, and then converted, correctly, it must be said, into visual representation, rather than through scientific study, and then, of course, there is Christ himself, and perhaps even his mother Mary, because maybe she shouldn't be called a person but something else, someone divine, but there are a hundred or more figures squeezed into it, thirty below, the stokers and their companions in the dark boiler room, the dark basement of the *Ayuntmiento,* the City Hall, and perhaps twice as many, I mean, perhaps more than twice as many, in heaven, in the messy space above, a tumult, no, not twice as many, but perhaps a little more than below, more than thirty, so a total of maybe sixty or a little more squeezed into that tight five by three meter space, don't feel like counting, it'd be hard to do it anyway without putting your finger on each of them, saying the number, and moving ahead, so, it's pretty tight, although heaven looks airy compared to the basement below, with empty gray space here and there, but what a tumult, great static tumult there in spite of the actual tightness! Christ in the very center, apex, zenith, no, not zenith and not apogee either, just apex, the high-point in the center, above, toward whom the unborn soul is directed, pushed, Virgin Mary at his feet below on the left, that is on his right, the emaciated anchorite Saint John the Baptist with an animal pelt around his loins, facing her, Mary, across the birth canal, the opening of the birth canal, she, ready to receive the partially formed creature, and he to channel, to direct it to the Father/Son, to Christ, who presumably will turn it into a fully-formed, a well-formed, child-soul that ultimately presumably will turn into a handsome adult male figure, then there is on the left, on Christ's right, below, Saint Peter with the keys, two of them tied together with a string, dangling precariously off the spread fingers of his right hand, his elbow resting on a cloud,

and then on his, on Christ's left, also below, the biggest
tumult and tightness, squeezed together, perhaps two dozen
human shapes, with Saint Paul as the second figure, then
further to the right, smack in the center of the first row, the
silver-haired and silver-bearded, popeyed Spanish emperor,
I mean king Felipe Segundo, Philip II, kind of strange his
being there, I think, because he was still alive when the
painting was finished and died ten years later, in 1598,
anyway, then way on the right, St Thomas, the patron saint
of the church, of Santo Tomé, with his big carpenter's
square, and in-between, or rather here and there, a whole
bunch of others, among them, supposedly Mary Magdalene
and Mary's companion Martha, both of whom at the same
time I just now and often can't find, as if they had left the
picture together for a bathroom break or an intimate woman-
to-woman chat in the private, that's about it, although
actually not quite, but anyway, when did I see it, the painting,
The Burial? first, I saw it with the second one, of course,
since I came to Toledo with her first, and after that I saw it
with the first one a few times, each time we came to Toledo,
and alone? alone, no, I mean, I never saw it alone before
coming here this time, I never came to Toledo alone before

that, and the painting always stayed in my mind, big and beautiful like a *flamboyán* tree, huge, with dark green leaves and these bright red flowers all over it like bleeding wounds, no, wrong image, like flames, the flowers like flames, like little fires that'd burst out all over it spontaneously and together, spontaneously and simultaneously, out of vivacity, out of joy, *flamboyán,* flame-buoyant, buoyant flame, magnificent, yes, yes, but no, no, wrong again, that's not it, that's not the painting, that's a memory from Mexico years later, the painting big, true, yes, big and sharp, clear, bright, with light, green light like a giant emerald, beautifully cut emerald in the middle, where the count's body sags, and it, the green light and the count's body are reflected in the armor of the knight leaning over him on the left, over the count, as if in his, in the knight's heart, in his soul, reflecting, conveying the sadness he feels at the count's passing, at his being dead, beautiful, absolutely beautiful, but it's wrong again, not my memory, I mean, not my memory now, but then, wrong of course, for the painting isn't like that at all, there's no green light in the center or anywhere else for that matter, but red, I mean, red and yellow mostly, and it's not the person leaning over him, over the count that's wearing

13

an armor, but the count himself, and the reflection is in IT, in his armor, and it is that of the person leaning over him, it's actually two of them, one on each side, but that's not important here, is immaterial, so it's actually ass-backwards, the other way around, I mean, what I thought then the painting was like and what it really is, but it's still beautiful, just as beautiful, almost, essentially the same, a person reflected in another person's body as a sign of compassion, sadness, the painter having transcended his craft, his goal of rendering reality, creating a faithful image, and becoming an expert on the nature of man, an explainer of life, a poet, and I just couldn't get it, couldn't get that image out of my mind, and it haunted me day and night, not leaving me alone for a moment until I finally had to give in, so it was it, the painting, that made me come here, it and my memory of Spain, the love I bore it, but why the green light when there's actually only red and yellow? curious, strange, probably because I like it, like green color, the color green in general, always did, spring, renewal, plants growing, sprouting leaves, green leaves, *Verde, que te quiero verde, verde viento, verdes ramas*? yes, perhaps, very likely, I think, partly so at least, Lorca's poem and Spain, but emerald? for the same reason, I mean, its color, emerald-green, of course, but the cut? rectangular with a large flat surface? hah! amazing! could it have   something to do with the engagement ring? the engagement ring I bought for the woman I married, the first one, with a big green stone which was supposed to be an emerald, but turned out to be a fake, made of paste, and eventually disappeared somewhere because of disuse, because of the stone, the paste fake becoming all scuffed up and worn around the edges? I was cheated, of course, but the store went out of business and I couldn't sue it, but that's a separate story, anyway, but the ring? the ring contributing to my thinking of there being a green light that looked like a giant, beautifully cut emerald in the painting? very likely so too, undoubtedly to some degree, but that's not all, I'm sure, we are mysteries to others and at least, actually even more so to ourselves, anyway, the painting, they say El Greco shed his Mannerism in it, it's true, but not quite, there are some figures, like up in heaven, and the images on the vestments of the two saints below that carry, display those characteristics of Mannerism, elongated bodies, distorted, waving like reflections in water, swaying like flames in the air, but the rest, in particular the faces of the nobles, the stokers, they are realistic, very realistic, are considered great realistic portraits of the Spanish notables, of the Spanish, Castilian *hidalguia,* nobility of the time, but to me they also look Expressionistic, reminiscent of German Expressionism, not quite, but close to it, their overwhelming sharpness, clarity contrasting with the vague, hazy rest, acting like exaggeration in German Expressionism, yes, to me it seems as if the painting was done by a sixteenth century Spanish equivalent of Otto Dix, or Emil Nolde, or Beckmann, what's his name? don't remember right now, it doesn't matter, Max, yes, his first name was, is Max, so, or Max Beckmann, and I think that it has been suggested by others that Mannerism bears resemblance, affinity to Expressionism, elongation, reflection-like waving, flame-like swaying expressing the painter's feeling about the subject with the aim of making an impression on the viewer, you express in order to impress, yes, it was that day, in the morning, I think, yes, in the morning, as I was alone in the house and was sitting on the sofa in the living room, taking a brief, two-minutes rest after my exercises before having my usual spartan breakfast of a bowl of salted cooked oatmeal and water, that I looked at the things around me and saw them different than normally, same, but different, beautiful, but more so, surprisingly beautiful, the flowery oriental carpets, rugs, the big, matching pictures, paintings on the walls, the hand-made, made to order, wooden Spanish furniture, much of it with *cuarterones*, the raised squares, made out of hard Galician chestnut wood I was told was guaranteed to last four hundred years at least, shining, the furniture shining here and there like bronze, the bronze chandelier over the long, narrow dining-room table, an exact copy of the one hanging in Felipe Segundo's, Philip II's alcove, bed chamber with a window overlooking the altar of the chapel in El Escorial, so that he could hear the mass said three times a day as he lay in his big four-poster bed, dying, a view like that, I'm referring to myself sitting on the sofa in my living room and looking, so a view like that from room to room, two, no three of them through the open doors like in Velazquez' *Las Meninas*, with the reflection in the mirror, beautiful, beauty, order and beauty I took years, it took me years, some sixty years to assemble, to put together, and then I realized, realized for the first time that this was my heritage, this was what I was going to leave behind, and suddenly it felt so small, beautiful, but small, pitifully small, but still my own, my own count's palace, manor house, on June 27, 1431 the Polish king Władysław Jagiełło signed over to a Hungarian or Wallachian count the ownership of my mother's hometown and the surrounding villages, which was transferred to three of his sons, who took the names of the places they owned, the last name of one of whom my mother carried, and on my father's side too there were counts bearing his last name, and therefore mine, so a count of sorts I may be, am, and suddenly I couldn't bear it any longer.

3

IT'S MORNING, I think, but it's still dark, not very, not black, not pitch-black, but gray, dark-gray, dark charcoal-gray, more like dusk, more like late dusk than morning, but I'm pretty sure it's morning, and not too early, mid-morning it must be, typical, typical for this mute, charcoal-gray city, charcoal-gray town, finally I'm out in the square, in the little *plazuela,* and make a beeline toward the church, trace out with my footsteps at a sharp angle a dotted line, a bisectrix across the open space, pass through the door, they let me in without stopping, they know me, the *forastero, extranjero,* an Albert Camus and Collin Wilson stranger who comes every day to stand in front of the painting for a few minutes before leaving, unchanged, there are people in the church, but it remains empty, some vague shapes, figures in the empty chapel too, yes, dark charcoal-gray city, town, there are six torches, six big torches burning in the painting, shown burning in the painting, in the lower, terrestrial space, part, the boiler room, basement, dungeon of the *Ayuntamiento*, the City Hall, one between the first figure on the left and the gray-hooded Franciscan monk, who, that is, the first figure, the man in question, not the Franciscan monk, it has been suggested, is Juan López de la Quadra, the master of the building of the church at the time the painting was done, and second one, a second torch above the man, who is apparently Diego de Covarrubias, the elder brother of El Greco's great friend Antonio de Covarrubias, who is given lots of space further to the right in the painting, squeezed in, that is, the head of Diego de Covarrubias squeezed in between the Franciscan monk and the black-habited Augustine monk, who's gesticulating with his right hand toward the Franciscan one, at whom he is looking, a third one, a third torch, just on the other side of the Augustine monk, above a face that is barely visible, the two torches, that is, the second and the third one, forming a pair and being companions to a pair on the other side of the painting, on the right, that are framing a strange head of a man looking up with one eye, a very pronounced left eye that seems to be made of glass, skyward, at the tumult above, and one more, one more torch, the last, the sixth one, almost directly under the first one and being clearly it's companion, its counterpart in the vertical direction, held, that is the sixth torch held carelessly and as if absentmindedly with his lowered right hand behind his back by Jorge Manuel, El Greco's young, seven? or ten? well, somewhere between seven and ten, so, held, the sixth torch held by El Greco's eight- or nine- or ten-year-old son, because he was born in 1578 and was eight when the picture was started and ten when completed, 1586 to 1588, so six flaming torches, but they cast no shadow, I mean light, they cast no light in the tenebrous space, seem to serve no purpose, that is no intended purpose, although they certainly serve the purpose in the composition of the painting, balancing the emptiness and fullness of the space on the left and the right as well as in between, and do it very well, and, interestingly, they are not red or yellow as one would expect, but white, pure white like the white collars and jabots, I mean, ruffs of the figures in the painting, and are sheer, translucent too, like the surplice or whatever you call the vestment that Pedro Ruiz Durón, the auxiliary priest of the church, way on the right, is wearing over his black cassock, and look, the flames look very much like the hands of the figures in the painting who gesticulate with them, as if communicating with someone, someone above, I would say Christ, or someone not in the painting, that is the viewer, or more likely both, in deaf-mute sign language, that is, the hands looking as if they were communicating in deaf-mute sign language, going left to right in the top row, the fourth figure, the Augustin monk, with his right hand, the nineth figure, the knight of Santiago, with both of his, the twenty-second figure, Pedro Ruiz Durón, the auxiliary priest, also with both of his, and finally below on the left, El Greco's son with his left, his left hand, his right one, although visible, holding the torch, rather than gesticulating, so it's six and six, six flames and six hands, clearly related, thought out, balancing off each other, and they, the flames, they cast no light, being like a luminescence equivalent of sign language, of deaf-mute sign language, that is a sign language of light compared to that of sound, we arrived in Spain on June 6th, June 6th? yes June 6th, landed in Brussels on June 1st, picked up the car, the VW notchback that gave me so much trouble later, well, not so much, gave me some trouble, primarily because they didn't market it back home at the time, and never actually did, it wasn't a good model, anyway, so, we landed in

Brussels on June 1st, the car, Belgian lace and chocolates, night spent in a dive that looked like the one in the painting of Rimbaud where he is recuperating after having been shot by Verlaine, the room we stayed in did anyway, dark and shabby, a flea bag, a bedbug bag, my forearm, the left one, the one I kept under the pillow, in the morning tattooed on the inside with bedbug bites, little red dots, lots of them, itched like hell for days, on to Pars, Hotel Alsina on Montmartre we'd taken a liking to, visit with her girlfriend from college Bettina, always made me think of Goethe and Bettina Brentano, was German but had an Italian-sounding last name too, von something, but Italian, not sure, but as I recall, well-off, father a diplomat, posted in Paris, she unmarried, lived with her parents,   lunch, nice, white fish, Pouilly-Fumé, green salad before chevre, then desert, *fraises de bois*, wild strawberries with *crème fraiche* probably, it was the season for them for sure, Notre Dame, La Sainte Chapelle, jellied   *consommé Madrilène,* one afternoon at Café de la Paix, at Le Grand Hotel, I'd stayed in for six weeks years ago, love jellied *consommé Madrilène,* was reliving my past, retrieving nuggets of nostalgic memories, so, two nights in Paris, then on to Brittany, Saint-

Malo, I think, buckwheat Breton pancakes with sausage and hard cider, a quick drive through Rennes and Nantes, rushing, no time to sight-see, night spent in a little hotel on the coast, near La Rochelle, don't remember anything except white furniture and the whooshing of the sea waves heard through the half-opened windows in the middle of the night, next day on to Bordeaux, another quick pass through, not much to see and didn't want to drink wine, too much driving, a boring drive along the straight road through Landes, lunch at a roadside inn with *foie gras*, and then Biarritz, with white spectral hotels, where we spent the night and I ran on the beach on arriving and which I years later saw in Romer's *Le Rayon verte*, crossed the border early in the morning into Spain at Hendaye/Irun, learned within minutes, when I asked the customs guy for directions, you don't use *camino* for highway, that's archaic, poetic, but *carretera,* a tiring four-five-hour drive along the winding coastal road through San Sebastian, there was no mention of Donostia at the time, just the beautiful saint's name, then Bilbao, and finally we were there, early afternoon, at 2 or 3, so, Brussels one, Paris two, New Rochelle and Biarritz one apiece, for a total of five, and the arrival, six, yes, it was June

6th that I, that we got there, I parked the car in that little park with palm trees near the post office and got the message, the other one's, the second one's message, *poste restante,* general delivery, as I'd done in Paris and would do from then on as I travelled for a few years, either from the first or the second one, depending on whom I was with, so got the message while she, the first one, stayed in the car, she, the crazy bitch, the second one, was already there, ready to sink her teeth, claws into me, but I wanted it, I wanted it, so she's not the only one to blame, the hotel was right there, near the park, the post office, so I decided to do my duty, screw her, she, the first one, saw me as I stepped out, stepped out of the post office, watched me silently through the closed window, her head turned right, she knew what was going on, I didn't want to talk to her, to cause more pain to her and myself, so, pointed with my finger at the hotel, it was a big building right on the corner, Bahía, Hotel Bahía, I think, it was called, moved my lips silently, saying I'd be right back, she turned her head away, she understood, accepted, I walked quickly to the place, went in, in a few minutes I was in her, the bitch's room, one of the floors above, took the elevator, a quickie, a real quicky, a tumble on the edge of the bed, skirt raised, underwear removed, hardly a word said, a kiss maybe or maybe not, what do I mean, maybe not? a kiss of course, prior to the rest, but a short one, a bothersome formality, don't waste your time, get it over with, then a promise to see soon and out the door, the elevator, back in the car in minutes, maybe ten at the most, silence, in the car silence, what else? silence, of course, and next? what in hell did I, did we do next? the hotel? we checked in at the hotel? the same hotel? I don't remember, must have, where else would we have gone? knew of no hotels in town, but that's impossible, that would have been too cruel, I couldn't, wouldn't have done it, it would have been a mess, I would remember, impossible, wait, wait, now I remember, a pension, a dive or almost a dive too, with lousy food, where we stayed for a few days, but no, no, that was in winter, with lots of rain, wind, OK, OK, that was after we came back from Madrid, where we thought we'd spend the winter, but didn't like it there, couldn't find a decent place to stay in, and stayed, stayed in the pension, for a few days before we found that beautiful apartment, a whole top floor in a private home, with a magnificent view of the beach, the beaches, out of that round tower with windows all around and a couple of armchairs to sit in, from which I would watch for hours on end rows upon rows upon rows of white-horsed Tatar cavalry attacking the defenseless land, yes, but where then? where did we stay when we arrived first? Roma! Hotel Roma! Rrrroma, as they pronounced it, yes, off that little park out on the ocean side of town, a nice place, nice little room, all white too, with a white balcony, good food to boot, soup, you would ladle yourself into your plate out of a tureen for lunch and dinner and my *te, pan tosatado, y dos huevos pasados por agua, cuatro minutos* in the morning, a very nice place, before we found that place on the ground floor at *doña* Marina's, where I brayed all night like a burro who's finally discovered who he really is before taking next morning my first trip through Spain with the second one, but the pain, the guilt! on, and on, and on! the bitches! both of them! they were in a league, in cahoots with each other, had something in common, hatred for me, the first hated me for my loving the second one, and the second one for my loving the first, female bonding they call it, and it came out at the end, the first one left me after I left the second one, it's well known that women bond naturally unlike men, men are stallions, all alone, always alone, fight off other stallions, fight to death, to guard room for their sperm, to propagate their genes, women are mares, coalesce into herds, a part-time stallion is better than no stallion at all, but I didn't want it! I didn't want it! all I wanted was to love you, to remember your face like a lilac bush in bloom on the corner of a dark street, to carry in my mind the sweet stain of your kiss.

4

THEY ALL KEEP silent as they walk past me, and even their steps make no sound if I pretend that I don't hear them, although mine stay on, I mean, stay loud, make a sound, like they're supposed to, the street twists this way and that, trying to get out of the tightness it's gotten itself into, out of this lack of space, this throng of buildings, this town, also without making a sound like a long, flexible creature, on the back of which I ride, ignorant, it ignorant, unaware of my being there, synergism, it's called, I think, you have all those barnacles riding on the backs or maybe also sides and even bellies and flippers of whales, on their skin, spending their whole lives there, and so it is with me, will be with me, that is, will be with me for the rest, for what's left of my life, I mean, not staying on the back of this street, but living in this town, because that's why I settled in it, came here, the mouths of people I see in restaurants and cafes I walk past move, open and close, but make no sound, of course, no surprise there, but still, I go inside one of them, a café by all appearances rather than a restaurant, it's nearly empty, only a few of the tables out of maybe a dozen or so are occupied, I sit down at one close to the window, there are some couples, nobody speaks, or if they do, it's as if no sound was coming out of their mouths, the people on the sidewalk passing by make no noise even if they open and close their mouths, of course again, but still again, the waiter appears next to me after a while and stands there mute, waiting for my order, I speak, as always, ask for a cup of *infusión de manzanilla,* to make sure it won't be confused with the sherry as it used to be when I first came to this country, it's too early for that, but more importantly, it's not the time to bring into this gray place *el sol de Andalucía embotellado*, bad taste, bad artistic taste, wrong, clashing element in the composition, gloom, doom and gloom all around, he, the waiter, walks away without saying a word, comes back a minute later, well, actually more like four or five minutes later, puts the small stainless steel teapot and the cup and saucer on the table before me, lays down the thin cash register receipt next to them, I wait, let the tea brew for a while, pour some of it in the cup, sip from it, it's boiling hot, burns my tongue, masks the taste of the chamomile, the *manzanilla*, but I detect it, *el olor de los campos de Andalucía infusiado,* it tastes good, I mean right, not bad artistic taste, not a wrong, clashing element, oddly enough, but no, why oddly enough, not oddly and not enough at all, the other one is linked, associated with gayety, joy, while this one, with hospitals, illness, *So, also hierher kommen die Leute, um zu leben, ich würde eher meinen, es stürbe sich hier,* it's dead still, mouths move near me and out in the street without making a sound, I sit, sip the healing, soothing liquid, empty the teapot, check the bill, lay down the money on the table, walk out without saying a word, mute city, city of mutes, that first time when I was in it the first time with the second one, and we sat in an open café in Plaza Zocodover, sipping beer, that is, I sipping beer, I don't remember what she had, so, as we were sitting in a café near that building pockmarked with bullets from the civil war, a group of guys, young men came along and sat at a table nearby, three or four of them, I think, not more, because the table would have been crowded and I'd remember that, and they sat there, not saying anything just making these funny gestures with their hands as if chasing away or trying to catch flies, annoying flies or mosquitos, speaking, communicating in sign language, and I thought they were deafmutes, a bunch of deafmute friends who'd come to the café for a drink, but when the waiter came, they spoke to him normally, I mean talked to him, ordering their drinks, I think all of them or certainly almost all, for it wasn't just one ordering for the rest of them, or even just two, and it was clear it wasn't like only one of them was deafmute for I would have noticed this, and when the waiter went away, they went back to their sign language, chasing away and catching flies and mosquitos, must have been members of a club or something, practitioners, admirers of sign language, appropriate for a mute city, for the city of mutes, but it may have been also for privacy, for the sake of privacy, so that no one would hear them, no one would hear what they were saying, which, I must agree, is a valid reason, but still, and in the painting too, they're mute, the row of stokers are all mute, mute of course because sixteenth century paintings, oil paintings, like all oil and other kind of paintings, don't talk, but I don't mean that, I mean, that they are shown, painted mute, all, I think, all with their mouths shut and looking this way or that, and some of them are actually gesturing as if in a sign language, as for instance, the fourth guy in the row of stokers, the one in a black habit, an Augustinian monk, I believe, addressing himself to the gray-habited Franciscan monk on the left, I mean on his right, saying with a graceful gesture of his right hand, something like, What's the matter with you? It's like this, that's all. Don't you see? Accept it, and another figure, another man, three or four, or maybe four or five figures to the right, that is to the left of the Augustine monk, a knight of the order of Santiago, Saint James the Great, marked with the big red cross of Santiago on his black tunic, doublet, on his chest, like the one Felipe Segundo, the emperor, I mean, king Philip II painted with his own hand on the chest of Velazquez in the latter's *Las Meninas*, knighting him for the painting after the fact, so, that man, the knight of Santiago, gesturing too, this time with both hands, extremely graciously, courteously, as befits a courtier, a knight of Santiago, saying something similar, like, That's the way it is, fellows, that's the way the ball bounces, the way of all flesh, so, accept it and move on, live, anyway, all of them keeping silent, all figures in the painting, all stokers, in spite of bursting with feeling, no, not bursting, something less dynamic, pregnant, yes, all of the figures in the painting in spite of being pregnant with feeling, with something similar

to thoughts, keeping silent, not saying anything, staying
mute, being unable to put into words what's inside them,
Wittgenstein put it neatly, succinctly in his *Tractatus, Wovon
man nicht sprechen kann, darűber muss man schweigen,*
What you cannot speak of, must be left unsaid, but El Greco
knew it and said, I mean, painted it four hundred years
earlier, more than four hundred, actually, let's see, 1600
minus 1586 is 14, plus 21 is 35, so it's four hundred and
thirty-five, four hundred and thirty-five years earlier, yes,
because El Greco signed the contract to do the painting in
1586 and Wittgenstein published his *Tractatus* in 1921, so
he, El Greco knew it and started painting it four hundred and
thirty-five years earlier, for how can you put into words the
way you feel about your own death? because that's what all
of them, all of the men in the picture have on their minds,
knowing what's going on below, and I don't mean, feel in the
normal sense, you feel bad, terrible, of course, that's the
secondary effect, but I mean the primary effect, how your
flesh and blood, and bones, and nerves, and so on, feel
about themselves ending one day, not being there,
decaying, putrefying, turning into dust and then
disappearing, vanishing, being blown away like dust and

leaving the surface clean, for they know this and they feel this, but it's not the kind of feeling you carry in your mind, your soul, it's something on the cellular, perhaps molecular or atomic, subatomic level, the awareness, or rather the state of being transient, terminal, endable, capable of being ended, of being nothing in the end, dust, ashes that will be blown away, and that's what the men, the stokers in the painting carry inside them as they witness the event taking place before them, but, *serán ceniza mas tendrá sentido polvo serán, mas polvo enamorado? yes*, shades of that, shades of that in me, well, actually, more than shades, a lot, a whole lot of that in me, of *sentido* and *amor*, not yet in *ceniza* and *polvo,* but ready to go, to move there when the proper time comes, as soon as she, the first one called that she'd arrived, I dropped the other one and ran, literally ran to the hotel or pension she was staying at and spent the night there, I think I spent the night there, I wouldn't have gone back to the other one, couldn't have, wouldn't have lasted, did so the next morning, got my things, said good-bye, I think, I'm pretty sure that's what I did, she, the first one was in the dining room, eating, I joined her at the table, didn't eat, but spent the night there, explained to them we were married, next morning, we moved to the parador at the Alhambra, stayed there for a few days, the splashy sound of water rushing down the *cuesta de Gomérez* as you go up it, hidden among the black-green vegetation on the sides, cruelly lavish in the bone-dry environment, golden fishes in the pool gulping water with their big fat lips, making me think of her mouth and therefore looking beautiful when I saw them with the other one a few days earlier, the thread-thin jets of water bending in over the Generalife pool like swords of comrades officer cadets crossed over our heads we never walked under while being married.

5

NO, NO, I didn't see it with the second one, I mean, I didn't see the painting the first time I was in Toledo, with the second one, that was not that kind of trip, art and tourism, a bit, perhaps, but mostly passion and guilt, a rush to get it over with, and I didn't see it with the first one many times either, just once, just one time, like perhaps the second or third time if we were four times in Toledo, something like that, but the painting stayed on in my memory like a big beautiful emerald ring, like that emerald engagement ring I got her, which turned out to be fake, I mean, the stone, it was paste, it was too late to go after that crook who sold it to me, he had gone out of business, or maybe died, don't remember, and replacing the stone was pointless by then anyway because the marriage was coming apart like a sleazy fabric in our fingers, yes, a big chunk of rock, giving off light like a green lantern being lowered into the grave by the two figures, reflected in their shiny armor, or at least in the armor of the one on the left, the other one not playing a role in my memory, but green, why green? don't know, for some reason green, I love green, Lorca's *Verde? Verde, que te quiero verde, verde viento, verdes ramas, el barco sobe la mar, y el caballo en la montaña?* partly, perhaps, but not so much, not wind and branches and boat and horse, but rather spring, rebirth, life, and the sea, the green waters of the sea, yes, but speaking of branches, *ramos,* I remember the fronds of a palm tree or some other plant I was standing behind in the patio of the *Alcázar* in Sevilla, Seville, we'd been passing through, me with the second one, on that trip, that painful trip, as we were walking through the different patios, and there was this French couple, I could hear them speaking French, young man and woman, about my age, both my age, and she and I had been throwing side glances at each other while passing, I, not because she was particularly beautiful, attractive, yes, although not exceptionally so, but because of my habitual practice of testing my masculine attractiveness, my sex appeal, and she because she apparently liked me, found me handsome, but this time, as I stepped out from behind that plant, she'd just stepped into the patio and our eyes met and stayed locked for a long time, five seconds or so at the least, and I knew I could have her, giving the right circumstances, situation, I could have her, and that was enough, and I moved my eyes aside as if nothing had happened, and walked past her, as she did herself too, both of us satisfied, I having made the conquest, and she having made the catch, but given the right circumstances, situation, it would have been tight embracing, and tongues in each other's mouths, and my groping down below, under the skirt, and she rubbing her hand on the hard mound through the cloth of my pants, both of us pulling off each other's clothes in an attack of madness, and so on, and so forth, it was really something, Christ! I was ready to do, was actually doing, doing virtual adultery on top of adultery, on top of ongoing adultery, youth, hormones, testosterone, an iconic manifestation of the male version of the human drive to procreate, to perpetuate oneself, to escape, cheat death, am being punished for it now, shuffling like that Italian guy in the camp who died either in that air raid or from malnutrition, but wait, a horse? yes, a horse on the mountain! when I, when we were driving to Seville, the first one and me next year or the year later, to the *Feria,* Fair of Seville, in April, early April it must have been, taking a

shortcut from Toledo through Talavera, Talavera de la
Reina, where Joselito was killed by that ferocious bull,
Bailador, Dancer, some dancer! Vaslav Nijinski of the *danse
macabre* kind! going on to Trujillo, a shortcut, a little country
road cutting through hills and fields, foot-tall grass and small,
hairy, brown, long-legged pigs feeding on acorns under the
short *alcornoques*, cork trees, on cresting one of them, one
of the hills, God, what a view! a big hill, a veritable mountain,
smack in our facers, purple, solid purple, some kind of grass
or another, a plant blooming with purple flowers, the most
beautiful sight I have ever seen! I think the scent too, like
lilacs? don't remember, probably not, probably just
freshness, just fresh early spring clean, pure country air,
anyway, we didn't make it to Trujillo that night, next morning,
it was too far, holed up for the night at a hostel run by nuns,
in a women's monastery, a convent, just off the road we were
taking, old, beautiful, like all churches, ecclesiastic
structures in Spain, they made us park the car, the VW
notchback, in a church on the grounds, a chapel in late
Gothic style, abandoned, not used, but in perfectly good
shape, state of repair, it was weird, gave me pleasure, at the
time, a militant, practicing, atheist of the Sartre kind,

existence precedes essence, bullshit! death!, existence precedes death, the only thing of importance that existence precedes is death, the rest is silence, anyway, back to the topic, had dinner, supper, in the refectory, with the nuns, the two of us the only laymen, I mean laypersons, guests, don't remember what, what we ate, it wasn't anything lavish, culinarily outstanding, but also not spartan, meager, something normal, simple, nourishing, OK, for otherwise I'd remember, after the dinner we went to bed in our cell, this one spartan, clean, the sheets nice and coarse, linen, white linen, reminded me of my childhood, summer vacations at grandmother's, great, we made ferocious love after turning off the light, spiced up by the fact that by their, the nuns' standard, having gone only through a civil ceremony, we weren't married and therefore adulterers, that is, ferocious on my part, not sure about her, I think she was faking it sometimes, maybe always, some women do, it's easier for them, it's easy, female privilege, and the next morning, another repast in the refectory, breakfast, I presume, also simple, nourishing, OK, then on to Trujillo, where that illiterate, rapacious pauper genius conquistador Pizarro came from, bringing along a horde of similar half-starved,

Yuriy Tarnawsky

rapacious stone-hard *extremeños,* men from Extremadura, from an extremely hard land, no wonder, all stone and order, stern grayness shaping the people's nature, a statue of him, of Francisco Pizarro, in the main square, I think, of stone, I presume, think, and then on to flowery Seville, horse-drawn carriages briming with laughing, colorfully dressed people, transporting them in all directions, hoarse voices, castanets, and *palmeo*, handclapping on street corners, and women frapping up their skirts, promising much, but showing little, in sultry dances.

6

I'M DOWN IN the cellar, at the *Ayuntamiento*, it's dark as always, but I can see surprisingly well, it must be because I'm there and not on the outside, looking in, stokers, yes, there are stokers here, there must be soot everywhere, I have to be careful so as not to smear myself, the ceiling is low and I'm sure it's covered with soot, so I must be careful not to hit my head on it, not to get it on my forehead, they're standing in a row like always, but are moving, swaying in unison, at the same time, like rowers rowing, like slaves in old galleons, in Roman ships, singing in rhythm with their swaying, in unison, well, not singing, more like groaning, giving out a deep loud sound, a dark loud sound as befits professional stokers, something like Uuuuh! Uuuuh! Uuuuh! or Uuuup! Uuuup! Uuuup! like men trying to move something heavy or, more likely, haul it out from a deep hole, strange, you'd expect them all to be pulling on a rope, a heavy rope, but their hands are free, they're just standing there like always, side by side and sway in rhythm, in unison, it's like in classical Greek drama, on the stage, the chorus doing its dancing, the *parodos*, or *stasimon*, or *exodos,* whatever, I used to remember them all, was proud of it, but have forgotten now, don't care, it doesn't matter, it's not important, I push my way in between the men, the stokers, they don't resist, don't oppose me, let me through like clouds of smoke or dust, like clouds of soot, yes, that's it, like clouds of soot, it means then I'll be smeared by it, get it over my body, clothes, my head, face, hands and clothes, yes, probably, yes definitely but to an unknown degree, I should check it, see how badly I'm stained, dirtied by soot, what for? it's too late now, it's been done and I'll take care of it later, wash it off, and even if I don't, if I don't wash it off, it doesn't matter, I'm one of them now, one of the stokers, in fact I'm sure that I'm smeared with soot all over now like they and that I won't be able to get it off, to wash it off my head, and face, and hands, so what? it doesn't matter, I'm not going up there anymore, into the streets, the world, it's OK, it's fine, sooner or later I would have had to do it, to come here, to join the stokers, everyone does eventually, it's my time now, it's OK, it's fine, I'm curious what's this pulling, this pseudo, fake pulling is all about, move up front, to the very edge, there's a precipice there, not too deep, I peer down, two figures in black, two male figures, apparently two stokers, are lowering something big and round, the size of a human head, into a hole, it's, the thing's attached to two thick ropes on the sides, each held by one of the men, the hole is round and small and they are having a hard time making the thing go in, they're trying hard, moving the object back and forth, but it sways on the ropes and won't go in, and the men on top, the stokers above, apparently feel they're helping the two to do their job, strange, but they're probably right, they know, they've been here for a long time, not like me, a novice, it, the thing, the object, is not smooth, but rough and jagged all over, mostly white and gray, with some green shining through in places, it looks like a giant freshly-mined, uncut emerald, but suddenly everything changes, I'm somewhere outside, it's a cold bleak day, as it appears, right after it'd rained, and I am marching in a funeral procession, the hearse is right before me, a flat black wagon with four posts with silver fluting on the corners that support a flat black canopy, covered with black velvet with silver fringe hanging down on the sides, there is a low platform covered with black velvet in the middle of the wagon under the canopy, but it's empty, I can see just the back of the driver as he sits, dressed in black, high up in his seat, but know he's bareheaded, as he should be, and is holding a long thin whip in his hand, I can barely make out the outlines of the big shiny hind quarters of the pair of horses pulling the wagon, but know that there are actually four of them, four of the horses, all coal-black, and that there are clusters of black feathers tied together with silver thread, perched like crowns on top of their heads between the ears, I also know that there is a brass band marching up front although I can't see it, but I can hear it playing something slow and sad, must be Chopin's funeral march, I obviously don't see them, but I finally also know that there is a long procession of people marching behind me, it's someone very important who we're burying, the fact that the platform on the wagon is empty doesn't seem to have a bearing on it, in fact, it seems appropriate, I'm dressed in black and also, as befits the situation, bareheaded, there are two persons walking next to me, one on each side, pressed tightly against me, in fact, each of them have put their arm under mine, which are tightly pressed against my sides, this is because I'm holding something heavy in my hands, I'm not sure who the two persons are, so decide to check and turn my head right, it's my former wife, the first one, she's also dressed in black and has a black hat on her head with a black-mesh veil over her face, I can see her fleshy features which look fleshier and flabbier than normally, probably because of crying, her eyes look red, not surprised, my curiosity satisfied, I turn my head left, it's the second one, she also has a black hat on her head with a similar black-mesh veil over her face, her narrow face with the long thin nose looks paler than normally, probably because of the sadness she's feeling, she looks sad, the thing I'm holding is heavy and is hard to carry, I have to press it against my belly to ease the strain on my back, and because of being hard is slippery, I feel, any minute it might slip out of my fingers, I'm concerned about it, worry also what would happen if it fell down on one of my feet, the one I had out front, it could break it, cripple me for good, I keep on walking, I still don't know what it is I'm carrying and it preys on my mind and in the end decide to check, it's a huge green rectangular stone, polished and with beveled edges, it's a giant emerald, cut as a diamond, about a foot long and proportionally wide and thick, that's what we are burying! a giant emerald, God, that's terrible! I think, but instantly dismiss the thought as unimportant because I feel the stone slipping out of my fingers, they are wet, have sweated up from the strain, the damn thing is slipping out more and more, I'm losing my grip, another second, and it it'll be gone, and then it is, it falls, both of my feet momentarily are out front, I will be crippled for good, forever, God! I scream in boundless despair and at that instant wake up, with the charcoal-gray light of the Toledo morning forcing its way into my eyes.

7

EL ESPOLIO, **SOME** say, that is, some authoritative sources say, *expolio,* don't understand why, not in Spanish, to the best of my knowledge, comes from Latin *spoliare,* to spoil, go bad, which in turn comes from, comes in Latin from *spolium,* related to our, to English to spoil, the hide, skin, you tear off a dead animal, so *espolio,* the disrobing, the disrobing of Christ, taking off his clothes before crucifixion, was like skinning an animal that's still alive because even if the taking off of the clothes wasn't painful, probably wasn't that painful, psychologically it must have really hurt, he, Christ, knowing what was coming, and seeing on top of that how the henchmen were drooling while casting dice over his clothes, who gets what, who gets the better one, especially the beautiful red robe, don't understand why he wore it, how he got it to wear, he wasn't a dandy, rich, maybe someone gave it to him, some rich admirer, and he, not having means to buy himself a more modest, less conspicuous one, kept it and wore it, but perhaps also because of thinking it would make him more conspicuous, more authoritative-looking, or maybe his father, his super rich father, the multi-multi-multi trillionaire-zillionaire, the almighty, the all-powerful father gave it to him, to make him look more authoritative, a more persuasive preacher, advocate, proponent, agitator, instigator of the ideas he, Christ, was preaching on his, on his father's behalf, some father, some almighty father who'd do it to his son, who'd have him crucified alive and himself watch the beastly human freaks cast dice over who'd get the choices piece, the choicest spoil, the red robe after he'd been hoisted up, and all this for expiating his transgressions, sins against the human race, that is sacrificing his son to expiate his own sins, some expiation, he should have had himself crucified as his son looks on, bullshit, of course, nonsense, nothing of the sort, a clumsy, desperate attempt to patch up the hole in the theory, doesn't work, you see too well the stiches the idiots left behind trying to save their teachings, to cover their asses, in the cathedral, the painting, *El Espolio, The Disrobing* hangs in the cathedral, in the sacristy, much smaller than *The Burial*, than *El Entierro*, about three meters by two, whereas *The Burial* is about five by three, five meters by three, he, El Greco, started to work on it right after coming to Spain in 1577, and completed it two years later, in 1579, the other one, *The Burial,* nine years later, started it nine years later, and finished it in two, 1586 to 1588, a fast worker, fast operator he, El Greco was, had a son, Jorge Manuel, a year after arriving, in 1578, so must have started on him maybe three months or so after coming to Spain, working with, and on, I mean working first on and then with that local Toledo girl from a good family, Gerónima de las Cuevas that he for some reason never married, wasn't that uncommon apparently in Spain in those days, strange, a Catholic, a sternly Catholic country, well, why strange, apparently they looked at it in a different way then, he wasn't censured in any way, wasn't ostracized, and there are inconsistencies in societies everywhere, hypocrisies, but maybe there was a legal reasons for it, Spaniards were fond of lawsuits, notaries ruled the day, *Pleitos tengas y los ganes*, May you have lawsuits and may you win them, anyway, the painting, *The Disrobing,* looks to me like an exercise for *The Burial*, a cramped space, a bunch of faces, figures, packed tightly together, squished against each other, the action, the static action taking place down below, a workman, one of the henchmen bending down, looks like he's drilling a hole in one of the arms of the cross, probably a guide-hole for the nail to be driven in, and most importantly, a reflection in an armor, Christ's red robe visible in the armor of the man, the knight, presumably a Roman soldier on the left, on Christ's right, this one to me not as evocative as the other, the one in *The Burial,* which I always remembered as a beacon, a source of light, of green light, a huge diamond-cut emerald hit by a shaft of light in the darkness, this one, the one in *The Disrobing*, looks more like a stain, a red stain on a gray fabric, diluted red wine spilled over an unbleached linen tablecloth, I think there's something else spilled, I mean, reflected in it further down, below, something maybe yellow, don't remember, sort of smudged, unclear, anyway, and no heaven, in the painting, in *El Espolio,* there is no heaven as in *El Entierro,* nothing above, Christ, the only sign of divinity in the middle, in the center of the panting, going top to bottom, going down from nearly the top to nearly the bottom, and yes, the faces, the faces different, very different, from those in *The Burial*, different in *The Disrobing*, no decorum, no restraint of the Spanish *hidalguía*, of the nobility of Toledo, brutality, beastliness of the riff-raff of Jerusalem of the time, of the province of Palestine governed by the Romans of 33 AD, well, actually, as I recall, some of the faces look sort of decent, sad and pensive, and of course there are those three women at the very bottom on the left, Mary and maybe her sister, and also Mary Magdalene, I think, don't remember now, don't remember the facts, the bible, nor the painting that well for that matter, but the rest, the ones around Christ, anyway, beastly, characters from Bosch and Brueghel, from Hieronymus Bosch and Peter Brueghel the Elder, features twisted by heredity, by genes and greed, mouths open, eyes bulging, fingers reaching out to touch the spoils that soon might be theirs, but no Expressionism, in *The Disrobing*, as in *The Burial*, still, no Expressionism, Italian school, Mannerism and perhaps shades of Titian, I have read, anyway, enough, what was I coming to? the furniture, yes, the furniture, the Spanish furniture in the living room, dark brown, almost black cuarterones hit by a ray of sunshine piercing the dark air from the left, matter and shadows intermixed, a natural, organic, spontaneous work of art, ordered the furniture in Cabezón de la Sal, the place, town Concha Espina came from, Calle del Puente, number 9? not sure, something like that, *Muebles viuda* something, Hermanos Hermanes, I mean, Hermanos Hernandez? Fernandez? don't remember either, something like that, ending in "ez", maybe Gonzalez, anyway, the tall, younger one ran the show, the short older one a bit slow, I mean, less sharp, said *moscas de miel* instead of *abejas,* honey flies instead of bees, made the younger one angry, *Porqué lo dices?* hearing we were interested in bullfights, *tauromaquia,* sent us on to Tudanca, to see José María Cossío, way up in the mountains, He'll love to see you, loves visits from young people, *aficionados taurinos*, far, way up in the mountains, almost like in Tibet or the Andes, Machu Picchu, no, more like Tibet, the big stone houses with the red-tiled roofs seen from the car as we drove in, looking like houses in Tibet, I'm not sure if he, the tall younger brother called ahead, they were on good terms apparently, close friends, admirers of the academic, but José María, don José María welcomed us with open arms, I mean warmly, maybe even came out to welcome us, in which case the tall younger brother did call ahead, José María strange looking, in a black suit and tie, white shirt, but the suit old, rumpled, dusty, I think, the shirt not fresh, wrinkled, old-fashioned wire-rimmed glasses, sparse greasy hair slicked over the bald pate, a flabby face with limp warts on it hanging down like wilted vegetable or candles that melted in hot weather, was accompanied by a young man, his secretary, who didn't say a word during the whole hour-long, probably more than an hour-long audience, visit, a lover perhaps, could be, but maybe not, doesn't matter, of course, who cares, who cares now and I didn't care much then, had a live-in housekeeper, I think, I mean, I recall, an old woman, probably older than he, than José María Cossío, but much livelier, younger-looking than he, served us something, maybe *jerez,* no that was always at the Hermanos Hernandez, Gonzalez, whatever, maybe water, mineral water, Agua de Solares or Lanjarón, or tea, *infusión de manzanilla,* or beer, or red wine, *vino tinto*, yes, *vino tinto* more likely, to go with the red portable chapel he showed us, a family heirloom, I think, it looked like a palanquin, faded red fabric and tarnished gold, or perhaps it was a little carriage, yes, it must have been a carriage, with wheels, yes, it had wheels, it belonged to an ancestor of his, a military man, a colonel or a general, no, a general for sure, a scion of the Cossío family, I think, in the eighteenth or maybe even in the seventeenth century, no, not seventeenth and not the eighteenth century either, at the beginning of the nineteenth century, in the Peninsular War, fighting the French, and he took it along on his military campaigns.

8

HE, EL GRECO, The Greek, Domenikos Theotokópoulos, or Theotokópoli, or a couple more close variants of the latter, is apparently the eighth guy, the eighth figure in the row of stokers in the subterranean chamber, squeezed in tightly between the two grandees or whatever they are, between the two Spanish, Castilian *hidalguia* members or Toledo notables on his right and left, his face flattened, made narrow by their size, importance, looking straight out at us, at the viewer, the only figure to do so, which gives credence to the theory, the supposition that it is him, some have suggested other figures in the painting, one of them being the guy on his left who's making that plaintive, defeatist gesture with his white butterfly hands, That's the way it is, the way the cooky crumbles, folks! Nothing we can do about it, accept it and move on, live! but it couldn't be him, El Greco, he, the man on his left has that red cross of the order of Santiago embroidered on his black tunic, his doublet, indicating he's a

member of the order, which El Greco wasn't, notice also how
the man's right hand could almost as well be El Greco's,
raised, as if waving at you, at the viewer, saying, Hi, there,
it's me, El Greco, the man who did this painting, its author,
welcome to it, enjoy it, make yourself comfortable,   also as
if holding the paintbrush, painting, painting himself, his face,
he does a similar thing with the gesturing left hand of the
auxiliary priest Durón, Pedro Ruiz Durón, way on the right,
sharing it with the man standing in front of him, with Antonio
de Covarrubias, Covarrubias y Leiva, the famous humanist
and professor of University of Salamanca who in 1580
moved to Toledo, entered priesthood, and became Rector of
University of Santa Catalina, great fried of El Greco, whose
portrait, a solo portrait, El Greco painted, painted later,
perhaps two years or so, around 1600, and it also looks as
if the two, El Greco and Covarrubias, are gesturing toward
each other, saying hello, Hi, there, I mean, *Hola,* Antonio!
Hola, Domingo! El Greco pointing out this way the
connection, the close relationship between himself and
Covarrubias, perhaps, not certain, but perhaps so, it's not
that important, but perhaps, good artists do things like that,
don't miss the opportunity to display, practice their skill when

it doesn't distract, doesn't detract from the overall quality of the work even when it doesn't add that much to it, art, art and literature and music, it's the same, all kind of artists do it, anyway, back to El Greco, the eighth figure, he's fairer than all the others, has brown, brownish hair, a Greek, a fair-haired Pelasgian like the golden-locked Achilles, standing out among the black-haired Iberians, some of them with dark Moorish blood in their veins, also, down below him, below El Greco, way on the bottom, on the left, on our, on the viewer's left, stands his eight- or nine-year-old son Jorge Manuel, looking quite a bit like him, narrow face, long, thin nose, oval chin, like his father, all of which lends further credence to the theory, to the supposition that the eighth figure is El Greco, not that it matters that much, but it'd be strange if he didn't put himself in the picture, but did put his best friend and son in it, and if not him, if not the eighth figure, the eighth man, then who? he was reputedly arrogant and combative by nature, made fun of Michelangelo's *Last Judgement* when in Rome, said in public that he could dash off a painting like that in no time himself if needed, if the original were destroyed and people wanted to see another one like it, a bit like me, I must say, I mean, I, a bit like him, when I was young, when I thought I could outshine anyone, even Shakespeare if needed, why not? why stop at Sartre and Camus? what's so special about Old Will? Greek? was he combative because he was Greek? and me too? because I have Greek blood in my veins? mother said our, her ancestors came from Greece, but on the other hand, there is that document that says that the count we supposedly descent from was Hungarian, although his name didn't sound Hungarian at all, more Slavic or Romance, Romanian perhaps, more in the direction of the Balkans, and therefore Greece, so maybe that's why she said that we were Greek, God knows, it's not important, I mean, it's silly anyway, how could you preserve unaltered, unwatered-down genes of an ancestor of six hundred years ago, that's maybe twenty generations or more, silly, no way, and of course, not all Greeks are combative, how could they be? everyone would be talking about it, business-, trade-inclined, yes, but that's environment, culture, history, a maritime, to a large degree an island nation that prospered, grew strong as a result of trading, but being combative? all Greeks being combative? that's silly, stuck up, yes, he was stuck up, stuck up by nature, probably, and fueled by accomplishment, talent, which manifested itself as arrogance, combativeness, but he was young too, when he was in Rome, let's see, he was born in 1541 and came to Italy, Rome, I think in 1570, yes, 1570, so he was 70 minus 41, twenty-nine years old, not a teenager, not twenty, but young, pretty young, less than thirty, with some impressive accomplishment's behind him, so, stuck up, confident, overconfident, he was, yes, but who isn't stuck up and overconfident when he's young? I sure as hell was, boy, was I, and how! remember walking down the sidewalk one crisp, sunny, blinding-bright winter day, must have been a holiday or a Sunday, since I wasn't in school or working on a Saturday, smoke and/or steam rising, billowing out of a giant smoke stack of a power station up ahead and congealing in the crystal-clear cold winter air in these soft, rounded cubist forms balancing on top, I don't know, hundreds, maybe many hundreds feet up in the air, Christ, I told myself, if I would want to, if I would only want to, I'd lean back, take a few quick steps forward, and bound right over them, over the damn smoke stack and the cloud of smoke and steam above it, if I would only want to, no sweat, no problem, bah, humbug, as old Duck Chickens, I mean Chuck Dickens would say, and speaking of sidewalks, then, a few years before, and many afterwards, although not now, sure as hell not now and not quite a few before, sidewalks and show windows, their glass, eyes to the right, a slender lithe male figure with a mop of dark hair on top gliding by as if on water, eyes to the left, ditto, the same, a slender, lithe, male figure with a mop of dark hair on top gliding by as if on water, eyes straight ahead, a slender, lithe male figure with a mop of dark hair on top striding confidently forward, with the aim of stepping up and occupying its rightful place among the manikins in the show window, or a white towel after a bath wound like a turban around the head in the bathroom mirror, an Indian Raja, a sheik of Araby, a Rudolph Valentino, also in the bathroom mirror or in the rear-view one in the car, before starting up the engine or during a traffic stop, pouting lips and the nose curving down from the straining muscles, a Marlon Brando, Hey, Marlon! those two or three or five calls turned my head, made me really think it was he instead of me who was walking down the empty sidewalk after a late night session with Stella Adler as I was passing the door of the Actors Studio on the way to the Orchidia, even though it was ten years later, and he was already in Hollywood, and had gotten an Oscar for being Terry Malloy in *On the Waterfront*.

9

THERE'S A SURPRISINGLY large crowd of people here for such an early hour in the morning, an excursion tour, obviously, in a hurry to cover all that's on the agenda for the day, if this is Paris, I mean Toledo, it must be Wednesday, or something like that, from Portugal, it looks like, because they speak Portuguese, very loudly too, like a bunch of geese, what else would you expect from the Portugeese? Portugoose, Portugander, Portugosling, mostly women, but they're all small, and I can see without a problem over their heads, never noticed it before, the left hand of the man on El Greco's left, the first of the two knights of Santiago, the one who's supposedly the mayor of Toledo, looks like a jewel, a big diamond, surrounded by a bunch of little ones, a whole lot of them in a circle, as in a pendant or an earring, more like a pendant, actually, it's too big for an earring and it hangs down into the empty space between the two saints, St Stephen and St Augustin, the hand being the big diamond and the lacey cuff of the sleeve sticking out of the singlet, the small ones, gathered in a tight circle around it, amazing how these coarse little squiggles of white paint can look so much like lace, what a master, he, El Greco, was, is, still is and will always be, and not only because of lace, of all those lacey cuffs and ruffs in the painting, but the composition too, the placing of the man's hand where a wasted, empty place would have been otherwise, boring to the eye and the mind of the viewer, but to do it he had to invent a curious, defeatist gesture the man makes, referring to the situation, to the count's body being placed in the grave, That's the way it is, folks, that's the way the ball bounces, the way of all flesh, accept it and move on, live! but that's not all, to justify that awkward gesture of the left hand, he had to do something appropriate with its companion, with the right one, which he achieved by making it lean in the opposite direction, as if a mirror image of the left one, at the same time making it look like it could also be his own right hand, that is, the right hand of his image in the painting, raised as if to paint himself, great artist, yes, a great artist he was, way ahead of his time, did what modern artists, cubists dared to do only centuries later, like Archipenko did in his *Gondolier*, where a rod serves as the oar and the oarsman's leg at the same time, or as a squiggly line going down the middle of a face serves as the profile and also the full-view nose of a woman in many of Picasso's paintings and continues on below the mouth to end up as a cleft in the chin, well, actually, this is true of virtually all cubist art, all cubist works. where the artist breaks up the image of the subject he's painting into a bunch of flat surfaces and rearranges them, so as to produce a new interesting one, a new   image, some of them, some of the surfaces serving more than one purpose, function, having more than one meaning, so to speak, so he was a predecessor of cubism too, a predecessor of expressionism and cubism and maybe of something else, Portugal, in Portugal, I was in Portugal first when we went back home that first time, leaving at night, the ship slipping by stealthily, as if along the enemy's coast in time of war, lights in the distance shining like tears on a person's face, on our faces illuminated by occasional, distant lights, the stars, at least on mine, went down under the deck, into the cabin, unable to bear the pain, next day, Gijón, where I saw the first drunk in   Spain, staggering down the street, haggard and unshaven, as in New York, then the beautiful harbor of Vigo, where the woman, the attractive single young Spanish woman had tears running down her face, as she was sunning herself, eyes closed, stretched out in a lounge chair on the deck, probably on a trip to forget, as Gabo would say, *un amor contrariado,* a thwarted love, most likely an affair with an older, married man, sneaky encounters in an unpopular, out of the way café, like that couple I saw once while doing it myself, and occasional sex in the car on a dark street at night or in a hotel room during an infrequent business trip, and finally on, we finally on to Lisbon, Lisboa, Lishboa, the ship docked in the middle of the city, in the middle of a city miles away from the sea, went up the Tagus, Tejo in Portuguese, the Spanish Tajo that so tightly ensnares Toledo hundreds of miles away, earlier, docked near the huge suspension bridge that crosses the river in one long stride, everything black, here everything black, old women in long black dresses and with black kerchiefs on their heads, old men in worn, dusty black suits, sitting on benches on the sides of streets, black cypresses on a white hill swaying in the wind, little girls urinating in the open, their urine swaying like black cypresses in the wind, black language, with the clear, airy o always replaced by the black, closed u, *Tejo/Teju, Fado/Fadu, barco negro/barcu negru,*

Rodrigues/Rudrigues, went to a Fado joint one night, stayed two there, two nights in Lisboa, I think, it wasn't just one, for sure, and I'm pretty sure it wasn't three, so went to a Fado place one night, a *fadista*, a beautiful *fadista* singing, singing *Barcu Negru* among other songs, don't remember for sure, but pretty sure, I think, very popular, *Barco Negro*, extremely popular with the audience, with the tourists, especially, Amalia? was it Amalia Rodrigues/Rudrigues? Rodrigues/Rudriguesh? must have been, the alabaster complexion, the noble Roman nose, the chiseled high-boned cheeks, the short, wavy black hair, yes, I think so, yes, she, the first one, went up to her afterwards, suggesting she join us, me and her, in our hotel room for the night, what? am I crazy or something? what am I saying? in our hotel room? what hotel room? we were staying, sleeping on the boat, of course, and you couldn't bring a guest with you, nothing like that, nothing like that at all happened, and not Amalia Rodrigues either, of course, not the big star that she is, in some little out of the way joint, some other singer, don't remember, don't remember who, but someone young, of average skill and beauty, I think, for sure, for sure, so nothing of the sort happened in Lisbon, in Lisboa/Lishboa at the time, at that time or any other time we were there, and we were there two or three more times, no, just two more and three altogether, I think, yes, anyway, but something like this did happen, not with the first one, but with the second one, and earlier, back home, I got confused, mixed up, it was similar, but different, quite different, we went away for the weekend, the two of us, me and the second one, in another town, city, went out to dinner at a Spanish restaurant, we liked, all three of us really liked Spanish food, there was a show afterwards, a guitarist and a woman Flamenco singer, attractive, she, attractive, very attractive, looking quite a bit like Amalia Rodrigues, in fact, I expressed interest in her, expressed to the second one, my companion, and during one of the breaks, she, the second one, went up to her, to the woman, the singer, and proposed to her, suggested she join us for the night in our hotel, she, the woman, didn't say yes, but also didn't say no, left the possibility hanging in the air, apparently, anyway, she wasn't outraged, offended, I don't know why we thought it was possible she'd do something like that, she performed with a guitarist, and such teams are usually couples, but it must have been clear that this wasn't the case, the situation, don't know why, don't remember now, anyway, so, after the show, she, the woman, the singer just walked off, walked out, without acknowledging our presence, what'd happened, and we were, at least I felt I was, left with egg on my face, the nerve! the gall! to do, to want to do something like that, I didn't ask her, didn't ask the second one, to do it, for her to go up to the woman and propose to her, but must have expressed an interest in that, made it clear that I wanted it, disgusting! an adulterer conniving with an adulteress to commit more adultery! no wonder I'm here now and shuffle like that miserable Italian guy in the labor camp during the war as a punishment, upset, upset about it, about what we did then, about how I was, how I was back then, not only that event, but in general, what I, what the three of us were doing, need solace, something to relieve me, the painting, yes, but can't have it with all these Geese before me, filling up the chapel, gaggling, if this is Wednesday, it must be Toledo, shit! the damn Geese, they sure are taking their time, must have forgotten about it, but I must be patient, I must wait, any second now and they'll start moving.

10

I'M OUT IN the square, in the little *plazuela,* and make a beeline toward the church, trace out with my footsteps at a sharp angle a dotted line, a bisectrix across the open space, pass through the door, there's no one there to stop me, I mean to check me, to let me in, they must have stepped away for a minute to go to the bathroom, take care of some matter for a minute or two, will be back soon, that's fine, that's fine with me, I don't care, I head straight for the chapel on the right, it's empty, empty of people, that's fine too, that's pretty normal, but it's empty of the painting too! it, the painting's gone! there's just an empty white space there instead! that's scary! where did it go? have they taken it away? taken it to be repaired? taken away for good? it won't be shown anymore? I won't be able to see it? that's horrible, unfair! what am I going to do? I won't be able to exist, to carry on without it! I turn around as if to complain to someone, to ask for help, for an explanation, I'm just on the threshold of the chapel and can see all of the inside of the church, there's a bunch of people clustered around the altar, a throng, all men as it looks, dressed, all dressed in black, I'm intrigued, forget about my worry, my concern about the painting, the fact that it's gone, something in what I see seems to allay it, to allay my fear, concern, I push it out of my mind, head for the people, the throng, yes, it's as I thought, they're all there, the men, the stokers, they're there, it's they who have gathered there, that's why the painting is empty, they have stepped off it and have gathered in the church for a little get-together, for a little party, I make out the old-fashioned, sixteenth century clothes, the doublets, the white collars, stiff ruffs around their necks, the lacey white cuffs spilling out of the tight sleeves of their jackets, the puffy pants pushed into the tall boot of soft black leather, I'm glad, I'm happy, I will be able to meet them, to talk to them, to find out who they are, to learn their life stories, get some first-person information from the sixteenth century, wow! meet El Greco himself!, talk to him! find about his paintings! this one in particular! wow! wow! wow! I rush in their direction, walk toward them, toward the men, quicken my pace, want to be there as soon as possible, this very second, it seems to be a party, some of the men hold wineglasses in their hands, I mean, goblets, not glasses, not made from glass, from gold, golden, gold goblets, goblets made from gold or more likely gold-plated, they shine in the light coming down from the ceiling, contrast beautifully with the men's shiny black clothes, there's no trace of fear, shyness in me about joining the men, it's as if I know them, am part of them, part of the group, the coterie, the guild of stokers of Toledo, they'll welcome me with open arms as their own, as one of them, and they'll ask me how I've been, where have I been that they haven't seen me for so long, how is my family doing, and so on, and so forth, and it happens like that in fact, the first man I come to turns away from the guy he's been talking to, to see who it is that has stopped next to him, and his face brightens up instantly, his lips and features spread in a smile, *Hombre, como estás? Bienvenido, beinvenido. Hace mucho que no te veo. Donde has estado tanto tiempo?* he's holding his glass, his goblet in his right hand, moves the arm aside, puts his left arm around my shoulders, gives me a hug, an *abrazo*, and pats my back a few times, I do the same with my left arm, don't answer his question, since it's not necessary, and, smiling, ask him how he's been doing,

Yuriy Tarnawsky

Como has estado, hermano? Tanto gusto verte al fin despues de tanto tiempo, tanto gusto! I don't know who he is, don't recognize his face, don't associate him with any figure in the painting, but genuinely feel I know him, feel we are friends, feel that he is one of the figures in the painting, the fact I can't place him doesn't bother me, it's a small matter of no importance which will be resolved without any problem when needed, he turns toward the man he'd been talking to, brings his attention to me, we in turn embrace and exchange words of joy at seeing each other, other men in the vicinity are brought in in the same manner, I move deeper into the crowd, keep giving hugs and patting backs, have that done to me at the same time or in return, get sort of tired of it, remember El Greco, want to speak to him, ask where he is, *Donde está el? Quién?* they ask, *El,* I say, *El jefe, El Greco? Toto?* they ask, *Está aquí, Mira, Toto,* they say to someone in the crowd, *quien ha venido. Nuestro gran amigo, Hola,* the man says, *bienvenido,* stepping up to me, smiling, and extending his hand, it must be El Greco, Toto's apparently is his nickname, short for Theotokópoulos, how wonderful, I'm on intimate turns with them, will be, will be on intimate terms with the great one, with the one and only El

Greco, with one of the greatest artists of all time, wow! I step
up to him myself, we shake hands, he carries no wine goblet,
we throw both of our arms around each other, hug, gently
pat our backs, step back, each with his hands on the
shoulders of the other, look in each other's eyes, his are
penetrating, boring into mine like those of the eighth figure
in the painting at the viewer, he doesn't look quite like in the
painting, that is, not all the time, his face seems to change
like a puddle of water spreading on a table, now it's this light-
skinned, thin, elongated one like in the painting, now swarthy
and wide, looking like someone I've seen somewhere, it
doesn't surprise me, doesn't bother me, it's him, El Greco,
that's all that matters, he speaks some words in a strange
language I don't understand, must be Greek, I've read he
never ceased to be Greek, stressed it everywhere, wrote a
little note in Greek on a piece of paper sticking out of the
pocket of his son Jorge Manuel in the painting, I wish I could
say something in Greek back to him, remember the rumor
that my mother's ancestors came from Greece, decide to
mention this to him even though it apparently isn't true, but
you never know, so I say in Spanish that my mother's
ancestors came from Greece long time ago, he doesn't

comment on that, but smiles more broadly, his eyes light up, he stares at me even more intently, takes his right hand off my shoulder and raises it like the hand in the painting that's either the man's on his left or his own, my God! I'm all lit up inside, I think, he's going to paint my portrait, I'll be one of the figures in the painting! that's great! that's what I've been waiting for, what I've been dreaming of, what I've come to this city, to Toledo for! I've reached my goal! it's bliss! I can relax now, which I do, you need some wine, El Greco suddenly says to me in Spanish, he takes his left hand off my shoulder, steps back, turns his head left and says, Bring him a glass, Eulogio, I don't know who Eulogio is, probably a friend or an attendant, but almost immediately a young man, dressed like the others, steps out of the crowd, holding two big golden goblets in his hands, he gives one to me and the other one to El Greco, it's heavy, must be old, solid gold, is embossed on the outside, that is, is decorated with bas relief all over, looks more like a church chalice than a wine goblet, it's filled with wine almost to the brim, dark red, almost black, like blood, suddenly everything changes, El Greco disappears, and there's a movement in the crowd, nobody says anything, but people start forming a line, like a queue for something, it forms itself in the direction of the altar, hah, it's for communion, I think, we're all going to have Holy Communion, yes, of course, it makes sense, you don't have parties in a church, you go there for communion, I obediently stand in line, make sure I don't step ahead of anyone else, that I'll wait for my turn, I'm fairly close to the beginning, see the altar well, there's a priest standing on the edge of the steps, facing the crowd, he looks imposing, wears a miter and a huge golden robe, looks like the bigger figure in the painting, the older man, like St Augustine, who's actually the archbishop of Toledo, Gaspar de Quiroga y Vela, yes, we're actually not in the little Santo Tomé church but in the cathedral, in the immense, beautiful Toledo cathedral, people, the men, obediently step up to where he, the archbishop stands, open their mouths, he places a little white wafer on their tongues, they drink out of their goblets, swallow, stand still for a second or two, and walk off to the left, it's neat, you don't place your lips on a spot where someone else had put his, receive the communion, and then have more wine to drink someplace quiet, maybe chatting to a friend, sort of a party, a Holy Communion party, where you cleanse your soul and have fun, soon I reach the steps, it's my turn, I open my mouth close my eyes, feel the wafer being placed on my tongue, feel it start dissolving, bring the goblet to my lips, drink out of it and feel the pleasant sweet taste spread through my consciousness, then things change, I sort of swoon, start sinking, falling back, explain to myself it must be the result of what I've drunk, but that's OK, that's fine with me, I'll be fine, everything will be alright, I know that, and just then feel somebody's hands grab me from behind under my armpits, then another pair do the same under my knees, they hold me, lift me up, it's like the body of Don Gonzalo Ruiz de Toledo, the Count of Orgaz is being supported in the painting, and it must be the archbishop, Gaspar de Quiroga y Vela who's holding me up under my armpits, and yes, there was a young attendant who stood on his right, who must be holding me up under my knees, he looked a lot, actually exactly like St Stephen in the painting, yes, that's right, it must be them, the archbishop and St Stephen, who are holding me up, it's them, they came to my rescue, they saw me swoon and stopped me from falling down, from collapsing on the floor, but then a terrifying realization of what is actually happening comes over me, they, the archbishop and St Stephen are not holding me up, they are lowering me down like they are doing with the count's body in the picture, they are putting me in the grave, they think I'm the Count of Orgaz, but no, I'm not, I'm not the count, I'm myself, and I'm not dead, I'm alive, I'm not ready to be put in the grave, No, no! I scream, I'm not the count, I'm not the Count of Orgaz, I'm not dead, I'm alive, I'm alive! but then realize that they probably don't speak English, and so decide to repeat it in Spanish, scream, *No, no, yo no soy el conde, no soy el conde de Orgaz, yo no estoy muerto, estoy vivo, estoy vivo!* and at that instant wake up, it's night, dark all around, as always, barely any light in the room, the charcoal-gray ceiling stretches flat above me in the four directions, I'm in my bed in Toledo.

11

I'VE BEEN THINKING there're two knights of Santiago in the painting, but I'm wrong, I must be wrong, there's the tip, I mean, the end of the right arm of the red cross, of the emblem of the Order, sticking out from behind the miter of St Augustin, looking like it should be the left arm of the cross on the chest of the supposed mayor of Toledo, which you don't see in the picture, but it couldn't be because it's the right arm of a cross, I mean, because it's pointing in the same direction as the right arm of the cross on the chest of the supposed mayor, in other words, to the left of the painting, so it has to be part of another cross, which could only belong to the second figure to the left of the supposed mayor, the man leaning slightly back with his eyes raised to haven, although, physically, it'd be hard for it to be that, unless the man's doublet has slipped way down, it couldn't belong to the first figure to the left of the supposed mayor because he stands in the row behind the former and there's essentially only his head showing in the picture, and besides, he's too young to be a member of the Order, there's barely a trace of an incipient moustache on his upper lip, yes, I think that's what it must be, that the man with the raised eyes must be it, must be a knight of Santiago, given the situation with the extra right arm of a cross and the fact that he's in the very center of the painting, with a knight of the Order one space away on his right and left, given the constraints of the composition, El Greco had only this spot left for him to show that the man was a member of the Order, which he had to do, and it was probably for this reason that he left out the left arm of the cross on the supposed mayor's chest because it would have left no room for the said right arm to be put in, besides, he, El Greco knew, that an average viewer would be fooled into thinking that what was showing from behind St Augustin's miter was the missing left arm of the cross on the supposed mayor's chest, as I had been until now, a clever guy, a cheat, El Greco was, but a great artist, a Houdini of art, who could get himself out of any barrel he'd squeezed himself into, the cross, it looks like a dagger, like a *puntilla* they deliver the *coup de grâce, golpe de gracia*, to a bull who's been killed but refuses to die, he's on the ground, his feet under him, the head nodding or something, or on his side, in a puddle of blood mixed with sand, not yet dead, so the torero, the matador gets his *puntilla*, well, someone gives him the *puntilla,* one of his *cuadrilla*, team, a *peon*, subaltern, or more likely one of the *monosabios*, the smart monkeys, who's responsible for the equipment, the gear, don't remember what happens, too long ago, but the torero, the matador certainly doesn't carry it in his pocket or his waistband, especially since he doesn't have any of the former in his bullfighter's costume, the *traje de luces*, his suit of lights, anyway, so he walks up in a measured step to the bull, the *puntilla* in his hand, bends down, steadies himself, selects a spot in the back of the bull's neck, drives the *puntilla* hard into it, and moves it around a few times, so that it'll do its job, the bull's feet rise up a little in the air, trembling, as if the electric connection they need to function were loose, but quickly fall down and rest still on the sand, the cross, the Order of Santiago emblem, really looking like the *puntilla*, as I suggested? no, not at all, the former delicate and long, three of its ends baroque-flamboyant, looking like a *fleur de lis,* and the *puntilla* short and stubby, I think resembling the tip of the *vara,* the picador's lance, perhaps with a disk or a bar at the handle, the hilt, to prevent it from going in too deep, don't remember, too many years ago, and I saw it from afar, anyway, but wait, no, no disk or bar on the *puntilla*, on the *vara,* yes, to prevent it from sinking in too deep and hurt the bull too much, but on the *puntilla?* no, what for? it's supposed to go in as deep as possible to do its job, anyway, back to the *puntilla*, the *puntilla* pretty much black and the cross red, that is, the *puntilla* black at the start, although red after the fact, after the *golpe de gracia*, some *gracia!* mercy, *muchas gracias* for it, *muchas gracias por nada, de nada, de nada,* Christ! those Spaniards! always preoccupied with blood, blood and death, death in the afternoon, death in the morning, afternoon, evening, and night, twenty-four/seven, three sixty-five plus days a year, in the afternoons, before the bullfight, we'd take the trolleybus to the *plaza,* the *plaza de toros,* the car too problematic, parking and the traffic, the trolleybus easy, the stop a few blocks away from the house, the *entradas* we'd get during the week or earlier, as soon as the *carteles,* the posters went up, at the little ticket window in the center of town, a short, narrow dead-end passage near the central square, actually, a triangle, Plaza Generalissimo Franco, with the *Ayuntamiento,* the *Excelentissimo*

Ayuntramiento, the Best Fuck, on it, *sol,* always *sol, estranjeros,* hungry for the Spanish specialty, *el sol de España no embotellado,* cheaper too, a lot cheaper, not that *sombra* was that expensive, as was the case with everything in Spain for our relatively well-lined *estranjeros'* pockets, but frugality staying on, frugality picked up during the student days, and why pay more anyway? can spend the money on something else, there was nothing coming in, *sol* more fun too, more lively, the plebs, the working people, having fun, fun at the *fiesta nacional,* designed for that purpose, the place packed, teeming with people already, no matter how early we came, the street in front of the *plaza* was always full of people, mostly men, but women too, milling around, *hablando, charlando,* probably about the *cartel,* the bullfighters, who will do how, who's going to give whom *el baño,* the bath, I'd joke in front of *cordobesistas,* fans of El Cordobés, *Dicen que El Cordobés es sucio, que no se baña, pero no es verdad, cada vez que torean juntos, El Viti le da un baño, ha, ha, ha,* They say that El Cordobés is dirty, that he doesn't bathe, but it's not true, every time they appear together, El Viti gives him a bath, confusion, surprise on their faces, in their eyes, but no anger, saw the humor in it, acknowledged my wit, maybe even though they should have come up with it themselves, turned around, of course, reversed, although El Viti usually came out on top, killed well, very well, the best of his generation, and El Cordobés badly, Santiago Martín El Viti from the little village of Vitigudino near Salamaca, a classicist, a dour Castilian, and Manuel Benitez El Cordobés from Palma del Río in the province of Córdoba, a flashy, show-off *tremendista,* who was considered to have flopped if his belly wasn't covered with blood at the end of the fight, always stuck it out after the horns had passed, El Viti still as a statue, stoic with his *veronicas, pases de pecho, natural,* the sword would go into the bull as into a mound of butter, of soft butter, the bull would stand still for a second or two, as if deliberating what to do, but in the end would always hit the ground, sometimes with his *patas* sticking up comically in the air, pathetic! doubly cruel, dead and funny-looking, El Cordobés would often run around his, trying to stab it from afar, as if to put out a fire on the stove, his *peones* desperately flapping their apron-like *capotes* around him, hoping to distract the bull, but in the end he'd butcher the animal somehow, sometimes using the *puntilla,* I liked El Viti, and she El Cordobés, associated herself with him, with him being penetrated once with a bull's horn, lying on his back on the ground, it showed later, boy, did it show! if there was time, we'd go in for a *copa de tinto,* a glass of red wine, harsh as Spain, as its geography, its history, its language, spoken in the grrruff Castilian manner, a *copa* at one of the *tavernas* we liked, a big, dark, space, for some reason usually near-empty, standing at the bar, the ring was already full when we got in, people, people in the *sol* at least, mostly standing up, turned this way and that, talking loudly to others, sometimes far way, shouting over other people's heads, laughing, drinking out of the *botas,* jets of red wine like long translucent straws stuck in the throats through the gaping mouths, the fragrant smell of *puros,* of Cuban cigars, thick in the air, the *pasodoble*s, ta-ta-ta-da, ta-ta-ta-da, electrifying, bringing out the appetite for what would come like a good, stiff aperitif, *Giralda, Torerías, La Virgen de la Macarena, Gallito, España cañi, El Gato Montés, El Gato Montés* my favorite, perhaps because of the *gato,* cat, I like cats, am a cat myself, a placid, moribund, harmless tiger, a big-cat Count of Orgaz, the two *alguaciles,* officials, all in black, up front, on their horses, the three *espadas,* matadors marching together, stern, inscrutable, like three judges that will pass the verdict on the case, and you know what it's going to be, no leniency, no sentimental compassion here, just a formality, you're a bull? you've had it! the black ram's-head *monteras* pulled down almost to the eyebrows above the stony, Mount Rushmore faces, the *trajes de luces* beautifully outdated, attesting to the long history of the tradition, its importance, the silver, gold embroidery, the little pieces of mirror sewed onto the fabric, the *luces*, sparkling, doing their job, the chests encased in the short loose *chaquetillas*, left arms strangely wrapped in the *capotes*, as if broken, tightly pressed against the rib cages, the tight *talleguillas*, pants, their satin, clinging to the flesh, blatantly displaying for everyone to see what the men are made of, the legs in the incongruous pink silk effeminate *medias*, the feet in dainty flat black women's *zapatillas*, tragic black on the top and the bottom with effeminate eighteenth century elegance in between, the *cuadrillas* in obedient files behind each of the *espadas*, the picadors on their *peto*-ed, mattressed horses, the *monosabios,* with the teams of mules and the drivers at the end, the order is given, a clarion, I think, a clarion sounds, the gate of the *toril,* the bull pen opens, and he, the *toro*, the *moriturus,* dashes out, angry, furious because of what's been happening to him the last few days, runs around, boiling-mad, his tail curled up, his nostrils flared, his head raised high, horns flashings, eyes searching all around, Where is he? Where is that sonofabitch that's been doing it to me? Where is he? Come out! Come out, you, coward! Let's fight! Let's have it out here in the open, in front of everybody! Come out! lowers his horns from time to time, stabbing the air, threatening, See, what I can do, what I will do to you? Come out, you coward! Let's have it out! then a gradual simmering down, cooling down, cutting down to size, the *banderilleros*, the *picador,* the *matado*r with the *capote,* then the *muleta*, the crutch, some crutch! a small piece of thin red cloth, only it and the man's skill and wit against a mountain of rage and muscle plus two knife-sharp horns, with the *capote—veronica, media veronica, chiquelina, gaonera, revoltera, mariposa,* and so on, with the *muleta— pase natural, pase de pecho, pase cambiado,* and so on, the bull is confused, tired, finds his *querencia*, a spot where he feels safe, confident, stays still, the matador gets ready, aims the sword like a rifle, keeps the bull's eyes on the muleta, enters or provokes the bull to *embestir,* to charge,

Yuriy Tarnawsky

gets the sword in, sometimes all the way to the hilt, the bull suffers a little or a lot, or falls to the ground with its feet comically up in the air, either way winds up a lifeless heap of flesh on the ground, the team of mules gallops in and drags it away, exit the bull, the mess he left behind is cleaned up, the next one's ready to go.

12

WHO IS THE twelfth figure in the line of stokers, the second knight of Santiago with the cross of the Order that has slipped all the way down on his chest, on his doublet, only the tip of the right arm of which is sticking out from behind the miter of St Augustin? he must have been a man of great importance, since he is right in the center of the painting, the first figure just off the vertical line dividing it in two, surrounded on both sides by the other two knights of the Order, with exactly one figure between him and each of them, so probably more important, at least in the eyes of El Greco, than either, and yet, hard as I have tried, I wasn't able to find any mention of who he might have been, strange, strange even if someone did come up with a suggestion as to his identity, because it apparently isn't well-known, which it should be, but there are other significant lapses of scholarship connected with the painting, such as the suggestion that El Greco's brother is in it, that one of the knights of Santiago is El Greco himself, and that Cervantes is hidden somewhere among the stokers, so, perhaps, in the light of this, it isn't so strange that people haven't showed more interest as to who he might be, anyway, he, the twelfth figure, the twelfth man, is shown to be pious, perhaps the most pious of all personages in the main row, his head tilted left and his tear-filled eyes directed upward, heavenward, looking straight up the birth canal through which the count's soul is being pushed as it is being born, he is also the central and most expressive figure of the three who are pictured full-faced, looking up to heaven, the other two being the seventh figure, four spaces, that is, figures to his right, and the twenty-first figure, eight figures to his left, there are four more figures looking up to heaven, two in the row above, close to the center of the painting, clearly, of lesser importance, and two in the main, the twenty-second figure, the auxiliary priest Pedro Ruiz Durón, who is shown in profile, with his back turned to the viewer, and the twenty-sixth figure, the last one on the right, turned sideways, looking up strangely with his big left eye that seems to be made of glass, but none of them come anywhere close to expressing their feeling, as he, the man in question does, displaying his sorrow at the count's

death and hope he places in the latter's soul's salvation
when it gets to heaven and sits at the side of Christ, teary
eyes, yes, in Granada, I and the second one, we stayed at
a little hotel in the center of town on a narrow dark
passageway that fed into a street, there was a café on the
sidewalk right in front of it, a restaurant, actually, that may
have been connected with the hotel, yes, I think, it probably
was, it almost certainly was, we often ate there, breakfast,
breakfast always, and lunch and maybe dinner sometimes,
that is, usually, it was convenient, the food was apparently
good, we, I got to know a waiter, who usually served us, and
one day I started to talk to him about Lorca, those were the
Franco times in Spain, and people were careful about what
they said, you didn't criticize the government and avoided
talking about the Civil War in public, saying anything good
about the Republicans, the Loyalists, I saw a couple of times
men being hauled away by plain-clothed policemen in the
crowd gathered in front of the bullring in the town where we
lived, for apparently saying something unwanted, anyway,
so I started talking to him, to this waiter, about Lorca, and
he said, leaning close to me and speaking in a whisper, that
he was from Víznar, a little village on the outskirts of

Granada, and that he knew the location of the grave in which Lorca was buried, it was right in Víznar, he said, on the edge of it, but people were reluctant to talk about it because of being afraid of the authorities, I don't know if he was right, because to this day it's been maintained that Lorca's place of internment has remained unknown, but that's unimportant, I'm sure he wasn't lying and thought he knew the truth, he was probably referring to a mass grave where the people executed by the *Franquistas* were buried, in which Lorca's body may have been thrown, anyway, Lorca was in Granada at the beginning of the Civil War, going there for safety's sake and to be close to his family, which lived in Fuente Vaqueros, about twenty kilometers west of Granada, within days, was arrested by the Nationalist militia, and was executed soon thereafter, the uprising started on July 17, July 17, 1936, and Lorca was shot on August 19, barely a month later, as apparently always or almost always, this was done very early in the morning, before sunrise, and, the waiter said, Lorca was crying and pleading like a child with the militiamen to be spared, which they found despicable, making them angry and say, he should die like a man and not a *maricón* that he was, this, he waiter said, was reported by other prisoners, who had witnessed it and had been spared, on another occasion, I mentioned to this waiter I like Flamenco, and he gave me the address of a place in Albaicín, the former Moorish and now Gypsy quarter in Granada on a big hill you see so well from the Generalife, where they held *juergas* people could attend, wrote out the address on a slip of paper, and put his name on it, said, they'd treat us well, the place looked strange, more like a private home, a room in a private home, than a performance space, which it apparently was, that is, a room in a private home, with a long table and a bunch of chairs along it and against the wall, and something like a stove in the back, there were just a few people inside when we came, maybe three or four, we sat ourselves at the edge of the table and waited, more people kept coming in, maybe a dozen in total, a guy came around, put a *jarra de tinto* and two glasses in front of us and collected the money, not much, I think maybe 500 pesetas, about 3 dollars for each, we didn't show him the paper, tell the waiter's name, it clearly wasn't needed, a few persons, men and women, were milling about in the back, as if doing house chores, suddenly they coalesced into the performers, two female dancers, one male, a singer and a guitarist, both also men, and the performance began, it was good, quite good, but not as good as Agujetas and his wife Tibulina, la señora Tibú, the dancer, I saw years later back home, those were real good, especially him, but she was good too, very good for, I think, a Jewish woman from Brooklyn, surprising, why surprising? look at José Greco, I think, he was Italian and from Brooklyn too, raised in Brooklyn, an iconic Flamenco dancer, anyway, during the break a woman came around, looked at people's palms and told them their fortune, the past and the future, young, looked like she was in her twenties, she looked at mine, but refused to say anything, said it was confusing, unclear, she didn't want to tell me lies, it was obvious she saw something bad and didn't want to tell it me, I got worried, upset, kept asking her, but she wouldn't budge, looked a few times angrily at my companion, the second one, she knew what was going on, I wanted to pay her, but she refused to take any money, said she didn't tell me anything, but as she was walking away, she suddenly stopped, turned around, and said, *Porque querrás venir a Toledo un día para morirte? Mejor en tu propia casa, en tu país. Pero tú no vives en tu tierra natal,* she added, *No,* I said, *No vivo,* surprised, amazed, amazing she knew everything! that I would come to die in Toledo one day and that I didn't live in the country, where I was born.

13

CERRAR PODRÁ MIS *ojos la postrera somba*, I wonder if he, El Greco knew Quevedo, let's see, Quevedo? Quevedo, I think, lived from 1580 to 16 something, 1640's something, to 1645, yes, Quevedo lived from 1580 to 1645, the final shadow was able to close his eyes in 1645, and he, Toto, El Greco, lived from 1541 to 1614, easy to remember, leave 1 alone, of course, change 5 to 6, and reverse the last two figures, 41 to 14, so 1641, yes, but Quevedo was only six when El Greco started the painting and eight when he finished it, a child, a mere child, younger than his, El Greco's son Jorge Manuel, younger by two years, he, Jorge Manuel was born in 1578 and Quevedo in 1580, he and Quevedo could have been friends, pals, true, but no, Quevedo lived in Madrid, I think, and El Greco in Toledo, close, but still, sixty miles or whatever it is, one hundred kilometers, no, not quite, more like seventy kilometers, forty plus miles apart, but still, especially in those days, it would have taken four, five, six hours in a cart, wagon, postillion, whatever they used for getting around then, a good part of the day, a day's trip in each direction, but why would have El Greco known Quevedo, the boy? why would his son and Quevedo been playmates? Quevedo became famous for his writing when he was an adult, but later, perhaps, later El Greco could have known Quevedo after Quevedo became famous, or at least could have heard of him, but I don't remember anything of Quevedo's life, don't know when he became known, famous, he was thirty-four when El Greco died, so probably not, Quevedo probably wasn't so famous by then that El Greco would have known him or known of him, so, no, there's little chance El Greco ever knew Quevedo or even heard of him, he was ill in his old days anyway, so he probably wouldn't have followed who's famous in Spanish literary circles when he was old, but Gongora? did he know Gongora? *Oh excelso muro! Oh patria, oh flor de España!* probably, or possibly at least, Gongora was born in 1561, so he was twenty years younger than El Greco and lived till 1625, was twenty-five when El Greco started the painting and so was too young to be included in it, but El Greco probably heard of him later, he was interested in culture, literature, the arts, artistic life in the country, in Spain, he has Covarrubias, Antonio de Covarrubias y Leiva, the scholar, who was his friend, in the painting, and some have suggested Cervantes is one of the figures in it, although it's apparently not true, even though Cervantes lived in Toledo at the time, anyway, and *serán ceniza mas tendrá sentido, polvo serán, mas polvo enamorado?* they will be ashes, but ashes full of feeling, they will be dust, but a dust in love? her eyes, the second one's eyes looked like two aluminum wash basins, scuffed up and dented in places as we were saying good-bye when I come to pick up my things in the morning, I don't know when she left, probably the next day, there was nothing for her to stay for, we, the first one and I walked past her as she sat in a café, in a sidewalk café, in Zaragoza, a few days later, on our way back home, alone, she sat alone, huddling, bundled up in the heavy overcoat of solitude, she didn't see me, us, me and the first one, and the first one didn't see her either, at least she didn't tell me, and I'm sure she would have, I didn't tell her, of course, didn't mention the fact to her, guilt, pain in my body and soul! and the drinking of beer in the square, in Segovia, that capped it all off! a threesome! the three of us, out of the same glass, big, huge, almost a bucket, the waiter himself suggested and we silently accepted, although I don't think any of us wanted it, I certainly didn't, accepted as punishment, don't remember when, but not before, certainly not before, so it must have been later, bizarre, how this dragged on, went on and on, how I, the three of us could stand it, crazy, crazy what people do to themselves and others for no reason other than their own stupidity, she, the second one, had a cat, a skinny little female, all white, that was perpetually in heat, bled all the time, stained the sofa, bed, rug, there was something wrong with her, she seemed to see things that weren't there, would stare into nothing, turned sideways, her eyes big, the ears laid back, the back arched, would hiss, her mouth wide open, the teeth bared, then suddenly back off, slink away, defeated, meowing plaintively, and hide under the bed, I called her Juana la Loca, Crazy Jane, Juana la Loca, Joanna the Mad, Mad Joanna, a daughter of the Catholic Monarchs, Ferdinand and Isabella, married Philip the Handsome, Archduke of Austria of the house of Hapsburg, he died ten years later, in 1506, apparently from typhoid fever, she went crazy with grief after that, had his body embalmed or something and took it around with her all over Spain, after her mother's death became nominal queen of Castile and Leon but never really ruled, prevented by her father and Archbishop Cisneros, who was in charge of the government, in 1509 was committed to a palace-dungeon in Tordesillas, outside of Valladolid and stayed there until her death in 1555 at the age of seventy-six, kept the body, her husband's body with her, kissed it before going to sleep every night, had six children with her husband, four daughters and two sons, the elder one, Carlos, the future king of Spain, stayed with her for a couple of years until Cisneros had him taken away, it was said, he looked and behaved then like an animal, a half-starved puppy dog, because of living in the abysmal, filthy surroundings, we, me and the first one, stopped off at Tordesillas in one of our trips through Spain, on the way to Seville? the Seville fair? not sure, perhaps, probably, the palace-dungeon's gone, and in its place sits a convent, convent of Poor Clares, her one-time potential soulmates, sisters, but, as I recall, she didn't show any emotions, affinity for them, had put her Catholicism behind her, found other interests, me temporarily, to be precise, the throne in which the couple, she and her husband sat has been preserved and is exhibited, the heavy folds of the canopy hanging

over it make one think of the Duero, of the current of
the river Duero, which flows right nearby.

14

RECUERDE EL ALMA dormida, avive el seso y despierte, contemplando, cómo se pasa la vida, cómo se viene la muerte tan callando, Jorge Manrique, did he, El Greco know about him? know about Jorqe Manrique? about his *Coplas? Coplas por la muerte de su padre? Verses on the Death of His Father?* May the sleeping soul remember, liven up the brain and wake up, contemplating how life passes, how death comes so silently, maybe he knew him personally too? I mean El Greco knowing Manrique, did he know Manrique personally? Jorge, his son, El Greco's son was named Jorge, Jorge Manuel, but that's the same, essentially the same, so, maybe he named his son after Manrique, Manrique died in 1479 and he, El Greco came to Spain in 1477, two years earlier and started the painting in 1486, no, God! what am I saying? I'm off by one hundred years! Manrique died in 1479 and he, El Greco came to Spain in 1577, not 1477, and started the painting in 1586 and finished it in 1588! ridiculous! it's always like this, the brain's not working when you're asleep, when you're sleepy, half-asleep, as you try to wake up in the morning, that's why we get all these crazy dreams, he, El Greco couldn't have known him, Manrique personally, but his son? could he have named his son after Manrique? knowing Manrique's poem, liking it? yes, sure, but naming his son after him? no, it's too unlikely, too far-fetched, the poem he very likely knew and probably liked, he was into culture, into literature, he has all those literary and scholarly figures in the painting, like Covarrubias and some have suggested Cervantes, so he almost certainly knew of Manrique and had read his poem, but there's no sign it had influenced the painting in any way, as far as I know, no one has suggested Manrique is one of the figures in heaven, in the heavenly part of it, for instance, so why would he name his son after Manrique, no, the answer is simpler and, I think, obvious, Georgios, Jorge, George is a very popular Greek name, and El Greco was very devoted to his Greek heritage and so, gave his son that name first of all because of that, the two, the painting and the poem deal with different subjects, death, that's true, but the painting celebrates the miracle of the burial, two saints descending from heaven and reburying the body of the long-dead count, whereas the poem expresses the sorrow at the death of the father and extolls his virtues, Manrique eulogizes his father, praising his virtues and the life he lived, anyway, enough, this is what I was coming to, the dream, the dream I just head I'm in his, my father's hometown, no, in the town, the city he went to school in, it's morning, I'm walking down one of its narrow twisted streets with tram tracks running down the middle, there's momentarily no one around, no traffic, I walk down the middle, between the tracks, they shine like silver in the morning light, I'm in a hurry, I'm rushing, I have to get someplace, have to get there on time, have to do something that awaits me, I don't know what it is, but it's important, it's very important, I know that, I'm late, the street turns left just around a corner, it's just a few feet away, a second or two and I'm there, I'm out in the open, in a little square with a large building ahead, it's Santo Tomé, I'm in Toledo! there's a tall, slender, figure of a man walking toward the door, he moves fast, a second or two later and he has gone up the steps, he's almost passing through the door, it's my father! he looks like he did when I was little, he's in one of those elegant gray suits he used to

109

wear in those times, I want to be with him, I shout, Dad! Dad! Dad! he doesn't hear me, however, and disappears in the black opening, I speed up, run faster, soon reach the stairs, bound up them, enter the door, there's no one to stop me, there's no one around, the church up ahead is empty, is empty of people, my father's nowhere to be seen, I suspect he's in the chapel, he went there to see the painting, I turn right, run along the wall, reach the chapel, the entrance to the chapel, rush in, it's completely empty, there's no one around, fear grips my heart, I've lost him! I've lost my father! I haven't seen him for so long, saw him just a little ahead of me minutes ago, and now he's gone! I'll never see him again, will never get another chance! it's my fault, my fault! I walk on, though, and see something dark and crumpled lying on the floor just before the railing that runs around the tomb, I'm intrigued and walk on, it looks like a man's suit somebody has left lying on the floor, I come up to it, bend down, and pick it up with both hands, it's my father, it's his body, it's all that's left of him, I arrange the suit to better lie in my arms, my left arm is under the legs and the right one under the collar, it sags like the body of the count in the painting, I remember the tomb, look down over the railing, it's empty, that is, it's a hole, a pit, the stone slab over it is gone, it's waiting to be filled, it must be for my father's body, I should lay it there, how will I do it? I can't just throw it there like a piece of old clothing, it has to be arranged carefully, it's my father's body, I can't step in there, I have to do it, leaning over the railing, I step up closer, press my pelvis against the railing, hold the suit carefully in my arms, bend down, that's not enough, the pit is deep, it's bottom is perhaps three or more feet farther down, I'll have to do it, though, it's my duty, I lean farther and farther, I'm nowhere near the bottom, however, I'm leaning way down now, the suit falls out of my arms and lies in a heap on the bottom, I must arrange it, I lean out more and feel myself fall head first into the grave, I scream with despair and at that instant wake up, with the charcoal-gray light of Toledo dawn streaming into my eyes.

15

THE SEVENTH FIGURE to the right of El Greco, of the one suspected of being El Greco, that is, the seventh figure on his left, is clearly not interested in what is going on up front and below, in how the count's body is being buried, in the fact itself, he, the man has turned to the right, with his left shoulder to the viewer, tilted his head way back, and is looking straight up into the groove, into the canal through which the count's soul is being pushed by the fair-haired angel with a woman's face in the process of being born, one wonders how he, the man, ever got there, into the boiler room of the *Ayuntamiento*, among this crowd of stokers who have gathered there to see Don Gonzalo Ruiz de Toledo, the Count of Orgaz, being put to rest, being reburied, one may imagine that he was walking down the sidewalk, and then this big crowd of men came rushing along, and he was swept along with them against his will, and found himself, uncomfortable and peeved, in this dark place, but now has lost his anger because he has found something that has absorbed his attention, which he apparently finds interesting, one wonders how, well, one doesn't wonder, one knows for sure, he's there because El Greco's paintbrush has put him there, because it has ordered him to stay there and to adopt the position he has adopted, all this for the sake of drawing the attention, moving the eyes of the viewer from the tragic, the mournful, the sad event that's taking place below, on earth, so, of drawing the former and moving the latter up, to heaven, where the count's soul is being delivered, born, witnessing thus the process of vanquishing death, of going from dust and ashes to eternal banquet at the side of Christ, the Lord, but he, the man in question, plays another role, the role of being a companion of the figure on the far right of the row of stokers, the one who has his head cocked in an awkward, unnatural manner to the right and is also looking up to heaven, although nowhere near the birth canal of the soul, he's way too far to the side for that, is just looking skyward, heavenward, up into the upper part of the painting with his unusually large, pronounced eye that looks as if it's made of glass, and the man in question, the seventh figure to the right of El Greco, of the one assumed to be El Greco is needed for this, needed to be a companion of the man way on the right, because otherwise it would have been awkward to have just one figure in the painting looking strange, looking different than the others, you don't want to bring in a new element in a painting, in any work of art, be it visual art, literature, music, and so on, without having something else, another companion to support, to emphasize it, a companion, supporter, yes, so the figure on the extreme, on the far right is also needed to be the companion of the one on the other side, they both need each other because they are part of a whole, part of a unit, a unit of men looking up to heaven in search of succor, solace, proof that life is not as bad as it seems, feels, that a person doesn't cease existing when his or her body dies, turns to dust and ashes, but that it lives on as his or her soul in the eternal banquet at the side of Christ, the Lord, and the first figure looking up in a strange, exaggerated way, the one closer to the center, the seventh one to the right of the one who is thought to be El Greco, has two more companions with whom it also forms a unit, the two figures, heads on his left and right, the first one looking sadly but discretely down, and the second one also somewhat sadly and discretely up, whereas the center one, the man in question, is doing it in an emphatic, exaggerated way, so the three figures, the three heads, form a unit, a statement about the ways a person, how man may react to the burial of another one, that is, how one may accept one's death, one's physical death, anyway, enough of that, heavenward, roses were still blooming in December all over the place, in public gardens, squares, parks, globs of intense color, red, pink, yellow, white, high up on their tall stems, they cut them down in January or February so that they'd have a fresh start, would bloom more intensely in the upcoming season, in spring, I swam in the ocean in December too, no one on the beach, but it was warm, the water fine, not much colder than in the summer, and the sun warm too, the air a bit crisp, but fine, December 10, I think it was, yes, December 10, wonderful, we'd sit in a sidewalk café in town, late morning, noon, with the sun hot on our faces, the mountains, the Picos, way in the distance, on the horizon on the right, gleaming like giant rough, uncut diamonds, like gigantic mounds of giant rough, uncut diamonds, covered with snow, she, a coffee, espresso or *cortao*, or maybe *con leche,* I, a tea and a *bizcocho* usually, or those porous things like ladyfingers, which I'd dip in the tea before putting them in my mouth, where they'd dissolve quickly like snow, in deference to my temporary but never-ending gastro-intestinal discomfort, liked also a lot the *sobaos, sobaos pasiegos,* full of butter, but somehow with little or no adverse impact on my stomach, little squares, about ten by ten centimeters, four inches, baked in wax paper which peeled easily, leaving a thin layer of the cooked dough, which I'd scrape up with a knife or spoon and eat after consuming the piece, this not in a café, of course, I don't think they served them there, but at home, at home too, *pantortillas de Reinosa,* wonderful things, thin, like nuns' starched wimples, sprinkled with plain crystal sugar on one side, medieval-looking, something like what you'd seen in a Breughel or Bosch painting, in one of the peasant festivities, actually went there, to Reinosa one day, to buy some where they come from, they were great, actually, about the same as back home, great, we stopped off at a nearby Romanesque church I'd read about to look at it and take pictures, for me to add to the collection I was amazing, wonderful, just wonderful, a window in the apse with a male figure clutching a giant penis, pressing it to his chest like the trunk of a tree, facing a female one, her legs in the air, her sex spread, staring back in the man's face, eternal punishment for being horny,   saw lots of such, you

117

don't have to go to India to see erotic art, the medieval peasants of Europe were there too, loved and still do the Romanesque, modest in size, simple, but with feeling, earthy, personal, the Gothic refined, technically impressive, but cold, impersonal, it's modern free verse vs the sonnet, Romanesque, Santillana, Sanillana del Mar, the fortress-like Colegiata church of reddish stone with the magnificent cloister with arches that reminded me of the perfect fingernails on my father's hands, how can you have such delicacy on the hands of someone who is so virile? strange! anyway, we went there many times, it wasn't far, but I remember one particular visit, it was in the spring, probably early April, a beautify sunny day, the morning at the church, leisurely, taking our time, savoring this detail and that, relaxed, not a worry in the head, as no cloud in the sky, lunch in a nearby restaurant, in an orchard, a table set up under a flowering tree, apple, or pear, or plum, white like a girl dressed up for her wedding, an appetizer and a Paella, shrimp, and mussels, and clams, and chicken, and *chorizo*, the grains of rice big, yellow, almost translucent, swollen with olive oil, delicious, filling but not cloying, a *media jarra de tinto* and a bottle of Lanjarón for a chaser, just right, not too much, not so that we couldn't enjoy the rest of the day, then at two, Altamira, you could go there any time then, didn't need a reservation, I'm sure now you do, assuming they let people in, I actually don't think they do, not just anybody, the moisture from people's breath damages the art, makes it peal, crumble off the walls, stone, I know they've stopped tourists coming to Lascaux, anyway, what magnificent art, how expressive! the sides of the bison actually bulging over the rock they're painted on, as if real, you expect them to be warm and soft if you touched them, and the technique perfect, perfect for representing what's represented, we've grown more sophisticated, even smarter perhaps, but not better artists, more sophisticated, more skilled, but not better at what we feel, that's remained unchanged, anyway, two or so hours there and back to town, the village, a leisurely walk, reconnaissance through the always near-empty medieval streets, time to go home, she went to do some shopping and I stayed in the car, leaned the seat all the way back and stretched out, it was getting dark when she got back, dusky, I could see her figure in the rear-view mirror, stealing along under the tall trees, coming to the car, lights were already shining in some of the windows, one thing she bought was a wine jug, a big, glazed *jarra,* it had two lions rampant holding up a shield with *VIVA MI DUEÑO,* long live my owner, painted on it instead of a coat of arms.

16

THE THIRD KNIGHT of Santiago, that is, the one who bears on his chest, on his black doublet the red cross of the Order, assuming that the second one is the one with his eyes raised to heaven, with just the tip of the right arm of the cross on his slipped doublet showing, so the third knight, whose identity we apparently don't know but who must have been also a very important person among the *hidalguía*, the nobility of Toledo, I mean, of all of Spain, Castile, because of the place he occupies in the picture, close to its center, being the eighth figure to the right of the one we assume to be El Greco, has a strange expression on his face unlike any other from among the stokers, the figures in the painting, he seems not to be involved with what is going on below him, with the burial taking place, nor with what's happening above, with the soul of the count going to heaven to sit at Christ's right side, but wait, wait, no! what a clever guy that Greek, El Greco was! he doesn't let any opportunity, any chance to prove his mastery, to use it to his advantage slip away! that man, the fifteenth figure, the one in the upper row, who stands with his left shoulder turned to the viewer directly above the head of the third knight of Santiago and is looking up to heaven through the birth canal, watching the count's soul being delivered, born, may be viewed as an indication, a sort of cartoon, comics strip bubble, filled with text, standing for thoughts or words, indicating what is going on in his, in the third knight's of Santiago head, he knows of heaven, is thinking about it, about his possible salvation, but is unable to overcome his proto-Existentialist nature and stares blankly ahead with his unfocused eyes, dejected, depressed, sick of life, sick of being himself, a man, a human being, what's the point? what is the point of going on if one day what's taking place below will be happening to me? why go on? why postpone this damn thing and not get it over with as soon as possible, quickly, right now? down into the hole! start rotting, rot, turn to dust, vanish, be blown away! a proto-Existentialist, a sixteenth century Toledo version of a twentieth century denizen of a left-bank Paris café, like I in that photo, holding onto a half-full/half-empty glass coffee mug with my right hand, my head turned left, eyes staring out the window, blinded by the white light crashing in through the dusty glass pane, no, not quite, I in the photo, not quite, not pallid enough, not Paris, and not the twentieth century, the next one, he, the man in the painting, neither, not pallid, not pasty-faced, etiolated, healthy, swarthy, a bony face, high cheekbones, a soft moustache over the full red lips, a beard, a full beard ending in a Spanish goatee, black hair neatly trimmed, handsome? like me? I, like him? no, not at all, my hair, my hair at the left-bank Paris cafés times lighter, brown, not black, and more of it, less trimmed, the face fuller, no beard, and in the picture even more, even more different, no need, no desire to describe it, not handsome, in a word, I mean, in two words, anyhow, left-bank Paris café times, I strolling on hot afternoons along winding cemetery paths in my tight black suit, a matching black narrow tie under my chin, matching black pointy French shoes on my feet, the mind black too, just the shirt white, a bouquet of *flores para los muertos* in my hand to set them alight on your graves, welcome me, I've come to you without breaking the silence, I'll lie down next to you like a flower, a cut flower, with sticky liquid on its severed feet, welcome me, I'm one of you, not distant and not disobedient, Sartre, the name like a cathedral, because of Chartres partly, I presume, but also by itself, the savior, leader, leader? leader where to? into the grave, the earth, to rot there, food for maggots! a maggot! one of the two maggots, the revolting renowned not obscure Dioscuri, Bobsey Twins, Castor-Beaver and Pollux-Poulou, existence precedes essence! bullshit! existence precedes bad faith, worse philosophy! bad teeth, bad breath, bad faith, bad philosophy! existence precedes death, that's all it precedes, death! the first time we went to Paris, me and the first one, still young, both of us still young, just out of college, we went to the cathedral, the Sartre Chartres, there you have it, the Sartre Chartres! went to Les Deux Magots, to inhale the air, aura of the place, movement, vaguely hoping to see Sartre with or without Beauvoir, with a bevy of young boys and girls dancing around him like angels on the end of a pin, but no, he, they never came, never showed up, he and she, they both were busy with something, with themselves, their future, fame, didn't want to come, what for? and anyway they were too famous by then, it was too dangerous, they had to be careful, but so what? I wouldn't have come up to him anyway, wouldn't have done anything, too timid, bashful, wrote him a letter once, but he never answered, I grew slowly out of it over the years, out of Existentialism, like a teenager out of his clothes, but still tried growing a beard years later, when I was for more than a month in Paris on that work assignment, but not so much for Existentialism as to flaunt the rules, free myself from the yoke I'd placed around my neck, big deal! the only unshaven one in the lab, building, but still, different, after a week started itching, my face started itching, kept scratching it until it got worse, big red blotches showing through the stubble, almost bled, have a sensitive skin, shaved it off, shaved off the beard, what a relief! like opening the window in the room and breathing in fresh air, aaaah, at last! I'm a clean-shaven man, I was born to be clean-shaven, all out in the open, nothing to hide, too nice a face to hide, I was told once, that time in Paris, already no black coffee, no dark depressive cafés, good restaurants, good wine, good French cuisine, *Monsieur-Dame*, they'd say as we'd come in, me and the girl, woman, *Une table pour deux, s'il vous plait, tournedos Rossini, canard á l'orange, ris de veaux, homard á la termidor, crêpes souzette, des fraises à la crème fraiche,* my favorite, better than *crêpes souzette*, less cloying, nearly got sick from them once, too much butter, *chevre* too, *chevre* for desert, strange, but good, delicious, a log, piece of a log of ripe *chevre*, runny, like white, salty honey at the very end, delicious, anyway, no, not anyway, forgot jellied *consommé Madrilène,* at the beginning, before all those above, with a squeeze or two of lemon juice, two or three actually, always liked sour things, delicious on a hot day, delicious always, hot or cold, always delicious, anyway, now anyway, the girl, woman, Odile, Odile De Bressy, Cressy, Dressy, something like that, don't remember, half-French, half-Spanish, I mean, Chilean, father French, mother Chilean, spoke a quaint English, What a bore! What a bore! all the time, sometimes inappropriately, but cute, quaint, What a bore! grew up in Chile, on Isla Negra, knew Neruda, she and other children would sit at his feet while he told stories, read his poems, eating grapes, green grapes, spitting out the seeds onto his sweatered chest which stuck to it like a green pectoral, green map of Chile, got sick one day, I got sick one day while there, in Paris, sick with the trots, not used to, not immune to the Paris, European germs, E. coli, holed up at her place, apartment, she called a doctor she knew, a young guy, prescribed something that apparently helped because I don't recall being sick very long, spoke English, the doctor spoke

English, pretty well, What a beautiful boy, he said, seeing me in bed, peering out from under the covers, probably looking like Rimbaud in that picture from the Brussels hotel room after being shot by Verlaine, a boy? a young man, a young man in his prime, he was probably homosexual, never occurred to me then, took it as a compliment, straight compliment, not that it matters, mattered then, felt proud, confident, she came after me one day, crossed the ocean, but nothing happened, I saw her, but nothing happened, lost the taste for philandering, not so much for her as for philandering in general, also, Paris is one thing, but home something else, too close to home, too close for comfort, maybe I wasn't that bad? was like all men, all men who can get away with it, young buck, sowing his wild oats? no, worse, worse than most men for sure, have paid dearly for it, like that woman in the movie, played by the less known of the Redgrave sisters, what's her name? can't remember, Lynn, that's right, Lynn Redgrave, the old noodle's still there, still purring, amazing, I'm not maaarried to you, George! I'm not maaarried to you, George! and a white sheet of paper with, as always, a neatly typed block of text on it, left on a black Formica kitchen counter top on an early May late

Yuriy Tarnawsky

Friday afternoon, my skin crawling from the sound of my fingernails on the bedroom walls, the telephone hoarse from the calls.

17

A BOILER ROOM of the *Ayuntamiento*, of the Toledo *Ayuntamiento,* the City Hall of Toledo? no, more like a restaurant, a basement restaurant, a dark bodega where the guys have gathered for a weekly or monthly get-together, a men's cooking club, a *txoko,* in the Basque region of Spain, where the members delight each other with their cooking skills on a regular basis, trying out different dishes or maybe repeating their favorite ones, their specialties, which the others keep asking for, I think, perhaps popular in other regions of Spain, although not nearly to the same degree, not sure, anyway, Spain, the segregation of sexes, men and women going out separately, or sitting in separate groups when they come together to a restaurant, at least it was then, when I came here to live for the first time, not sure if still is, haven't been going out much now since I'm alone, just these couple of places where lonely people like me come for a cup or bowl of something warm as a stand-in, a simulacrum for human warmth, but back then, yes, I mean, during El Greco's time, when he did the painting, yes, for sure, men and women going out and sitting separately in restaurants, in fact, I'm not sure if women went out to restaurants, bodegas then at all, probably not, probably stayed at home, the decent ones stayed at home, only the loose ones, the sluts went there to drink, debauch with men, go for a quick stand-up job in the dark corridor, under the staircase, bent over, the skirt up on the rump, a two-minute quicky, dog-fashion as Joyce would say, and back to drinking, anyway, so the guys in the painting, the stokers, yes, they're stokers but also a bunch of culinary fans, gathered for a weekly or monthly session, where the dish being prepared is putting a body into the ground, a burial, not a culinary, a cooking club, but a funerary one, bodega, back then, when I came here first to live, there was a bodega we sometimes went to, Bodega del Riojano, a dark, cavernous place, but nice, excellent food, nice ambiance too, original paintings on the bottoms of wine barrels hung up on the wall, there was one by Picasso, I guess, when he stopped by and offered to paint something, probably came because of the food, was told to try the place because of its food, or was invited by the owner to come, who heard he, Picasso was in town, but no, no way, wait, Picasso didn't have to be in town for his picture to be painted on the bottom of a barrel, could have done it in France, as a favor, somehow, for some reason having felt he should do it, not for a fee, but as a favor, for it's not likely the owner would have been able to commission the painting, it would have cost a fortune, it was an oil painting, wish I could remember what it was, damn it! but it was a nice one, a typical Picasso, had a signature on the bottom, couldn't have been a fake, and yes, there's no way Picasso could have painted it there, on the spot, anyway, those were the years of Franco and Picasso was a commie, fled to France at the end of the civil war, painted a portrait of Stalin, so young and handsome, the bastard! both he, Stalin and Picasso bastards, anyway, and yes, of course, none of those paintings on the bottom of barrels had to be painted there, at the bodega, could have been done as a favor like the Picasso painting and sent in, there was one I liked a lot, the most, even more than the Picasso painting, in fact, I didn't like the Picasso painting that much, appreciated it but didn't like it, like all of Picasso's paintings, art, he was a creative genius, no doubt, but leaving an emotionally moving

impression is something else, so, there was one, one
painting I really loved, don't remember the rest, there must
have been at least a dozen, maybe more, a little boy, seven
or eight, perhaps ten, but delicate, small for his age, a tilted
landscape like the sea seen from a boat lifted up by a wave
for the background, there's a strong wind's blowing, messing
up his face together with the long blond hair, eyes like two
child's fists each clutching, no holding firmly but gently, a
beautiful blue bird, his mouth blue too, to go with the eyes,
biting into a slice of watermelon which until then had been
kept in a parrot cage, made me think of myself, my ten-year
old face blown together with my hair by the hurricane winds
of history, my fate, the food? the food at the Bodega del
Rjoano? strangely, don't remember, it was good, excellent,
I'm sure, but I don't remember the dishes, the taste, too
similar, Spanish cuisine is not as diverse as French, and not
as complex, I think, so the dishes don't differ as much from
one restaurant to another, but good, it's almost uniformly
good, so it's hard to differentiate between them, single them
out, but no, that's not true, I do remember certain dishes
which were outstanding, except for some reason don't
remember what it was I ate at the Riojano, except that I tried

to drink there out of the *porrón*, the carafe with the conical spout and got the wine all over my face and shirt and, I think, pants, bad aim and lack of practice, we'd gotten a *porrón* ourselves prior to that, but didn't use it often, preferred the traditional glasses, you can savor the taste better that way, swirl the wine round in your mouth, aerate it, saturate your taste buds with it, enjoy, rather than letting it go straight into the gullet and then down into the stomach, it's good for cheap wine, so that you don't have to put up with its rough taste, I used to call it liquid barbed wire, red liquid barbed wire, what would you expect from a bottle costing ten cents, when mineral water, a bottle of *Solares*, cost twenty-five, but no, at the Riojano, the wine must have been good, from a barrel, but good, it was just the tradition to drink out of the *porrón*, old Spanish bodega tradition, that's all, like drinking out of a *bota* at a bullfight, I tried that once or twice too out of politeness, when offered by a neighbor in *gradas, sol*, made a mess of it too, I think, everyone must have laughed, *forastero-estranjero*, good wine out of a barrel, yes! Blanco de la Nava, excellent, white, tasted like muscadet but better, more body, muscadet sometimes thin, like a piece of aluminum foil on your tongue, between your teeth, it was served, the wine, the Blanco de la Nava was served among other places at that café downtown, near the ticket office, bullfight ticket office, had it always with their club sandwich, excellent, the club sandwich excellent, the wine with it excellent, and the wine excellent by itself, a great evening meal, would go there to watch television and feast on the food and drink, did my poetic doodles, visual metaphors on napkins, the eyes on the TV and the hand with the ballpoint pen in it roaming by itself over the napkin, napkins, saved some and took back home, lost now, lost with the rest of my count's estate, garbage, junk, ashes to ashes, dust to dust, junk to junk, garbage to garbage, the way of all things, material and otherwise, the way of the world, universe, everything, the club sandwich, a fried egg or maybe two over a big slice of *jamón serrano,* lettuce and probably tomato with some kind of dressing, between two slices of square white bread gently toasted, I mean, gently fried in butter or oil, it and a small, *media jarra* of Banco de la Nava, a royal, I mean, a count's repast, evening meal, excellent *tapas* in a different nearby bar, cold shellfish, *gambas,* crayfish, *mejillones,* mussels, hot *chorizo*, and especially the juicy, succulent, cold tortilla Española, delicious, could make it a whole meal, usually with beer, Aguila or San Miguel, don't remember now what was popular then, and in the spring, in Madrid, my visits to Madrid, doctors and San Isidro, other, *fresas, fresas de Aranjuez*, wild strawberries, like during the summer visits to my grandmother's, and *asparragos, asparragos de Aranjuez*, white asparagus, big, thick like a man's finger, thumb, roasted or baked or boiled, don't remember which, soft as butter, so that you could spread it with a knife like butter, butter with that peculiar asparagus flavor that makes you urine smell of iron some people hate, but I love, the best meal, Savarin said, is boiled asparagus with some butter on it, a crisp baguette, and a glass of good white wine, yes, for sure, I don't know what wine they served I drank when I went to Madrid, but it wasn't Blanco de la Nava, but that was in the spring only, couldn't get it, the asparagus during the rest of the year, but gazpacho, yes, I think you could get it anytime, perhaps not anytime, I don't think, it's a summer, hot-weather soup, when tomatoes are available, although nowadays it's not a problem, I think you can get it anytime now, haven't tried it here yet, too cold, but maybe I should, maybe it'll put some life, some of the *joie de vivre* back into my veins, bones, soul, there are different kinds of them, of the gazpachos, I mean recipes, everyone makes it a little differently, what ingredients you have and family tradition, recipes, I like them all, the pale, delicate, almost orangey, as if with sour cream, to the blood-red, bull's-blood-red, but there are, is a different kind of gazpacho too, white, white gazpacho, gazpacho *blanco*, made with almonds instead of tomatoes, red, you puree tomatoes, add soaked white bread, vinegar, oil, and chilled water, white, you use ground almonds instead, serve it with melon balls or white grapes, *uvas,* good, refreshing on hot summer days, the same with red, *uvas*, you can have *uvas* with *migas*, nominally breadcrumbs but actually fried, soaked pieces of bread , simple, but delicious, prepared when you're in a hurry, and red gazpacho you of course serve with croutons and hardboiled eggs, sometimes the yolk pushed through a sieve, paella, a red and yellow mess, a culinary equivalent of an unmade bed in the morning, but delicious, the scents, flavors, streaming toward your nostrils with the steam out of the big round pan, as if out of the gaping mouth of some enormous wild but harmless beast, a tamed lion, remember, after a strong bull's-blood-red gazpacho, a broiled sage-covered steak served on a round wooden pallet with a groove around the edge to catch the juice, a wooden-handled knife with a triangular blade, such as you see in old paintings, for instance in one of Breughel's, to defend yourself against with, in one of the Madrid restaurants, delicious.

18

WHAT IS IT? haven't noticed it before, another sixteenth-century Castilian proto-Existentialist, rubbing shoulders, actually shoulder to back, with the other one, with the third knight of Santiago on his right, right in front of the figure whose head sticks up between him and the knight in the back? looking downward, but the other way, in the opposite direction, to the left, also downcast, dejected, at the prospect of what lies before him, no, a momentary lapse of attention, concentration on my part, he's not dejected, he's communicating with, actually mimicking as in a mirror image the expression and hand gesture of Antonio de Covarrubias, who stands to the left and a little in front of him, with another expletive, gap-filling head sticking up behind them, who, Covarrubias, shares his left hand with the auxiliary priest Pedro Ruiz Durón, the expression, the expression on both faces, of the man in question and Covarrubias, one of sadness, but acceptance, admission of the inevitability of what lies ahead of them, of everyone of us at the end, the two hands, the right one of the man in question and the left one of Covarrubias/Durón forming a unit, a composition, a companion piece of the one, the supposed mayor of Toledo makes with both of his hands, saying, as the other two do, bending, however, toward, rather than away from each other, avoiding by this repetition, That's the way it is, folks, the way the ball bounces, the way the cookie crumbles! Nothing you can do about it, accept it and move on, enjoy life, live! so here you once again see El Greco's mastery, one two-hand gesture would have been lonely, possibly interpreted as random, a fluke, a mistake, but two form a unit, emphasize, support, validate, each other, make the painter's, El Greco's message clear, yes, the two faces, the faces of the two men, the third knight of Santiago and the man in question almost the same, nearly identical features, beards, expressions in their eyes, on their faces, what cleverness, ingenuity, mastery! a genius, he, El Greco, a genius, great! enjoy life! I sure did, still do as I stand here drinking in the painting with my eyes, sucking in with their parched retinas, with the parched lips of my mind the drops of beauty of the painting, but the smell, the scent, the sense of smell I once had, when I was young, almost gone, not quite, for I still smell the scent, the odor of churros and chocolate, actually the unpleasant, almost sickening smell of hot oil in which the churros are cooked before being served, the smell I smelled as I walked down the narrow Toledo streets mixed with the cold December morning air as I was coming here, but not the same, my sense of smell not the same, not as strong as it was then, when I was in my late teens and for some, for many years later, until I realized one day that something happened, that that wonderful smell, odor, fragrance, I smelled each spring, I think, around the middle of May, for a few weeks, perhaps two, or three, or four, that the fragrance, which for a while I thought was just a feeling of joy, of *joie de vivre*, of joy at being alive, at being young and feeling spring, but was actually the smell, the scent, of flowers, of hyacinths in particular, even when there were no hyacinths visible around, so until I realized that I hadn't had that feeling, hadn't smelled that fragrance for quite a while, for some years, and that it was most likely, almost definitely, not because it was no longer there, was gone, but because I could no longer smell it, because my sense of smell had dulled, had gotten weaker, weak, I noticed, smelled it, that hyacinth smell first when I was around sixteen and began to think of myself as a man, when I had started to wear nice clothes, fashionable adult man's clothes, long wide pants that swayed gracefully as I walked, caressing my calves, legs, gray they were, gray with thin yellow, barely visible vertical stripes at some distance from each other, I found that yellow, that yellow and grey went well together, harmonized beautifully in an unexpected way, got myself a knit gray and yellow short-sleeved shirt to wear with, with the pants, then found out that white, white shirt with full sleeves went even better together with the pants, the other shirt too similar, OK, but not enough, no contrast, wore a gray wide-brimmed hat sometimes that cast too much shadow, too much black on my still child's face, wore it with the pants and a jacket, a sports jacket, don't remember the exact color, but I think it was a lighter shade of gray than the pants with some black and blue specs in it, closely spaced, however, I think, something like that, and then, that dark navy blue suit they got me, tailor-made, wow! with navy-blue suede shoes and the gray hat on my head, or without it, without the hat, my thick long dark brown hair like a cap on my head, even better, even better than the hat, no black shadow and more attractive, but that was later, when I was seventeen, pushing eighteen, I think, fell in love with the Wild West for a while, cowboy movies, found a bandana someplace one day, started wearing it tied around my neck, with a knot up front that looked like a bow tie, thought it was cool, a cowboy among city slickers, remember one fall afternoon, must have been late September, early October, sunny, warm, I walked along the road that led from where we lived toward the city, the tops of its tall buildings sticking up above the tree tops, the famous spire, the tall slender cathedral spire popping up from to time to time above them like a bird, a huge black bird playing games with me, the game of hide-and-seek, in the cloudless pale blue sky, there were pear trees growing on both sides of the road, the pears were ripe, fell to the ground, a smell of fermented pear juice hung thick in the air, wasps buzzing around, crawling in the grass, over the rotting pears, over the ripe pears, squashed on the asphalt, pavement, I would pick out the hardest, least ripe ones, to eat, would take two, bite into each, rub them together, and lick off the creamy fruit mush, savoring it like a delicious preserve on a piece of pastry in a fancy café, couldn't afford to sit in one at the time, imagined I did, but alone, not with a girl, a girlfriend, didn't fancy anyone among the girls I knew, nor did any of them fancy me for that matter, not as far as I knew, anyway, some handsome stud! handsome in whose eyes? my own? apparently, probably, but no, this was later, but still, a friend of mine said his girlfriends' friend, a girlfriend had the hots for me, would get wet between the legs looking at or even thinking about me, but anyway, I alone at the time with no prospects or desires, too bashful, too young then, a dreamer, always a dreamer, even now, have dreams about dying, I in this deaf-mute, charcoal-gray city, not fit for this life, for success, lost in my dreams, my mind, myself, had, I had the hots for Silvana Mangano, at the time, I think, had seen *Bitter Rice* about then, maybe a little before or later, what fantastic thighs! God! no, at that time still no, still didn't see it, it was in winter, later that year or the next one, no, must have been that year, later that year, I mean that winter, when the movie began to be shown outside of Italy, yes, what thighs! and that strange mask-like face with the two eyes of a scared animal looking out of it, the eyelashes trembling like black butterfly wings, beating like the charred wings of a burned butterfly in agony, died years later from cancer, married to Dino De Laurentis, had four children by him, they separated a few years before her death and she started divorce proceedings, but died after being operated, in Madrid, of all places, *Also, hierher kommen die Leute um zu sterben*, yes, *Anna,* the film *Anna,* saw it years later, when I'd lost my hots for her, which revived them, seeing the film revived my lust for her, those thighs and all, as a matter of fact, I remember clearly the smell of hyacinths I smelled as I stepped out of the movie theater after seeing that film, it was late at night, the black, starless, bottomless big-city sky overhead with the tall buildings all around me, spring, the air warm, and that smell of hyacinths in my nostrils, incredible, incredibly beautiful, wonderful, youth, spring, she moving through those dainty, sexy steps, raising her left leg behind her while bending down the right and leaning forward and to the left, absolutely alluring! *Tengo ganas de bailar el nuevo compás* makes my skin, mind tingle even now!   it's also in Tornatore's *Cinema Paradiso,* brought back the memory, memories years, decades later, memory of the film and memories of my being young, of smelling hyacinths, *Ya viene el negro zumbón bailando alegre el baión repica la zambomba y llama a la mujer, Tengo ganas de bailar el nuevo compás. Dicen todos cuando me ven pasar: Chica, donde vas? Me voy pa' bailar el baión!* it was actually sung by someone else, another woman, Flo something, as I recall, yes, Flo for sure, but don't recall the last name, but so what? so what it was sung by someone else? it was her, Silvana Mangano's dancing that did it, that stayed on, the flashing of those mysterious, scared animal eyes, gone! all gone! the way of all flesh! shit! died alone in a hospital in a coma, in a foreign country, she apparently suffered for a long time, read in a book about an Italian director, maybe Fellini, don't remember, a book by a journalist who interviewed her husband De Laurentis while they were still together, he said she wandered through the house silently like a specter, passing through doors and walls, a ghost of her former beautiful, sexy self, like a specter, apparently semiconscious from pain, why were they getting divorced while she was mortally ill? he married her when she was nineteen! four children! she bore him four children! what a fink! all men, people, men and women, are finks, me and mine including, a similar thing happened to Monica Vitti, her and Antonioni, she died of Alzheimer's and he didn't even attend her funeral, the fink! now, wait a minute, how could he have attended her funeral when he died fifteen years earlier? I think she didn't attend his, but they'd broken up some thirty years earlier, so what? she should have come to his funeral, should have come even though according to her he'd broken off with her, so what? so what, he'd broken off with her? anyway, it's their business, I mean, it's her business, it certainly isn't mine, enough, enough already, back to where I was going, of Monica Vitti, she became my other great love, and this when I was married, ostensibly happily married, another distraction, another stick stuck between the spokes in the wheel of my life, a mirage on the horizon to distract, misdirect the caravan, the traveler, with her it was *L'Avventura,* of course, that did it, that distracted me, distracted, misled many a traveler, many a caravan of biography too, amazingly similar to Mangano, that smooth mask-like face and the mysterious, frightened animal eyes, although the eyelashes different, normal, saw it, the film, with the one I was married to, one bright, sunny Sunday afternoon, an early matinee, as I stepped away from the box-office window, noticed on the sidewalk before me, on the clean, smooth concrete sidewalk, in the blinding sunlight, as if in a spotlight, a twenty-dollar bill, bent down and picked it up, has stayed in my mind forever, I mean the memory, not the bill, the memory of finding the bill has strayed on in my mind forever together with the film, with the name *L'Avventura*, with Monica Vitti's incredible face, with my being smitten by it.

19

ANOTHER EXPLETIVE, A gap-filler figure, I mean, head, there is another gap-filler head between the non-proto-Existentialist figure that rubs shoulder to back with the third knight of Santiago on his right and Antonio de Covarrubias on his left, there is actually a whole slew of them, maybe a dozen in the painting, no, not a dozen, maybe ten, let's see, one, two, three, four, five, six, seven, seven, yes there are seven of those heads in total in the painting, are they all just that? spaces filled with random human, men's facial features to cover up the charcoal-gray emptiness? to make the painting less boring, more interesting? no, certainly not all, some of them look like portraits, regular portraits with distinct facial features, no less accomplished than the other, fuller ones, except without the image below the chin, below the lower part of the face, that man, head next to Covarrubias, is certainly a portrait, his features almost as detailed as those in the full figures, the same is almost definitely true of the three rightmost of the four heads sticking up above the others in the center of the picture, who are quite detailed, but perhaps not the first one, the first one of the four, who's mostly hidden by the ruffs of the young man with the trace of a moustache on his upper lip and the one on his left, with his eyes directed skywards, and even more not the head barely visible between the fourth and sixth figure, with the flame above it, and likewise not the one between the twenty-third figure and the twenty-fifth, that is, the man who's reading in the Bible or whatever the book may be, who is the parish priest Andrés Núñez de Madrid, the visage, the head in question pretty much hidden by the shaft of the cross being held by the twenty-third figure, twenty-third man, yes, these are almost definitely space fillers, just space fillers, an attempt to make full, solid the row of the stokers, of men, attending the ceremony of putting the body of Gonzalo Ruiz de Toledo, the Count of Orgaz, into the ground, for otherwise there would be just these two gaps in the painting, ungainly, ugly like two missing teeth in a row of otherwise perfect ones in a person's mouth, a gap, alone, yes, for a long time, I used to live alone, a long time? well, for a few years, how many was it? six, seven? hell, no, three! for three years only! amazing! it seemed like it was much longer, that's the kind of tricks psychology, I mean, your mind plays on you, it responds more to your feelings than to facts, anyway, so, for a fairly long time I lived alone in my big empty house, well, again, not empty, full of furniture actually, except for one room, one room, her former room, empty of everything, furniture and others, the rest just empty of others, people, the sound of my footsteps echoing in it, in the room empty of everything like sobs, like my sobs, which were desperately trying to fill it up, but the whole house, including the room, packed full with darkness when I'd come home from work at night, dense as concrete, the darkness dense like concrete, scary, tried to avoid it, postpone having to squeeze my way through it for as long as possible, would stop off at places to eat at times, to delay it, delay the pain of forcing my way through that dense concrete of darkness and emptiness of others, there was one restaurant I liked the most, a French, a French Provencal place on the top floor of a big department store, expensive, expensive the store and the restaurant, couldn't afford it all the time, besides, too boring, too monotonous all the time, would underscore, heighten the loneliness, would try other places too, don't remember any, not interesting enough, one maybe a diner, one of those in a shiny metal shell reminiscent of what they, diners, are supposed to be, railcars, I think, yes, railcars, one night almost there, at the French restaurant, changed my mind, drove to the hospital emergency room, What's wrong with you? Scared, scared of going home, Why? Don't know, it's empty, no one there, they brought in a doctor, a regular MD, I think, not a shrink, not a psychiatrist, I don't think they have them in the ERs, not enough business, need, anyway, he, the doctor was nice, calming, nice and calming, Why are you afraid? he asked, I don't know, I said, What's there that scares you? I don't know, nothing, there's nothing there, I think he was trying to weasel out of me something that might have given him the reason to detain me for my own protection, which may or may not have been true, that is, which was certainly only partly true, but was not the most important factor, so I started to pedal back, let the concern for my situation take over, reason triumphed, the fear went away, I reassured him I was OK, which I was, he was convinced, I thanked him, and they let me go, I think I had scrambled eggs for dinner that night, overcooked, as always overcooked, dry and white, looking like a Roman ruin overgrown with grass, had them, the eggs, standing at the black-topped Formica kitchen counter, the famous black-topped Formica kitchen counter that had a block of neatly typed text on a sheet of white paper lying on top of it one early May late Friday afternoon, with time dating began filling in the gaps, what dogs! one, a hoarder, a dog and a hoarder, had to step over rolled up Turkish rugs and picture frames in the hallway on the way to the bedroom, stepped into one of the latter, had trouble getting my foot out, didn't continue, turned around and without a word headed out, You leaving, you sonofabitch?! I ignored her, fumbled with the lock, managed to open the door, slammed it shut behind me, and rushed straight to the stairs, to the emergency staircase, almost diving head first into the stairwell, afraid she'd catch me in the elevator, sometimes I'd head to the wrong end of town, who the hell am I seeing tonight? had to go back, God! what loneliness does to you! would pick some up at parties, gallery openings, sometimes by giving them a kiss on the lips, which usually worked, one, at a gallery opening, young, which sharpened my interest, named Kobita, I think, no, not Kobita, Babita? no, Tabita? yes, Tabita, almost certainly Tabita, yes, a pale emaciated beatnik type in Gypsy rags, don't know what it was, potential or compassion that made me do it? offered to give her a ride home, didn't even make a pass at her, she was scared as we drove, looked like a mouse squeezed in the corner between the seat and the door, staring at me with her beady, unblinking mouse eyes, as if I'd rape her while we were driving or would force myself to her place after we got there and screw her, how? she said she didn't live alone, with her grandmother, I think, God! who'd want to get into your stinking tight little hole? nearly kicked her out of the car when we got there, was relieved more than she, then came concerts, classical music concerts, usually, almost always alone, much better alone, change, a change, a big, huge change, music swirling in the head, mind after coming outside like the stars in the sky above, swirling even in the dirty, light-stained city night sky, part of them, part of the music and the stars, the cosmos, no, not part, rather the opposite, a partner, an equal partner in the structure containing the music and the stars and me, spring swirling too, especially after church performances, Bach particularly, the passions, especially, always the passions, of course, Holy Week, Easter time, knew them, the two passions practically by heart, sadness like a curtain on the stage descending inside, tears rising at the same time in the eyes, as the performances were coming to an end like on leaving a place you love or saying good-bye to someone dear on the platform by the train, *Ruht wohl, ruht wohl, Ihr heilige Gebeine!... Wir setzen uns mit Tränen nieder Und rufen dir im Grabe zu: Ruhe sanfte, sanfte ruh! Ruht, ihr ausgesognen Glieder!* remember having crepes afterwards, French crepes one such time, with someone, I think, a woman, it must have been a woman, of course, don't remember who, not important anymore, I, self-sufficient, a partner with the music and the stars, a star myself, around which planets spin, would come home late at night, swathed in a tight navy-blue suit, white shirt with French cuffs, gold, silver, silver and turquoise cufflinks, a silk tie, one of many, a collection of maybe thirty-forty, more, striped, red white and blue to go with the navy-blue suit, polka-dot, white on maroon, the dots not circles, slightly elongated, squeezed together on one side, another, a matching one, white squeezed polka dots on a light blue background, others, a loose-fitting Missoni mustard-colored suit, serge,   I think it was, the material serge, beautiful, the jacket short, with wide padded shoulders, European-style, cool, cost a fortune, but I got it at a good price at that discount store, a red tie with human or animals figures on it, as I recall, magenta too, magenta-colored tie, other similar, similar colors too, to go with it, the suit, contrast with the yellow-mustard-colored cloth, and a white shirt, of course, with French cuffs, cufflinks and all, went walking once on coming home real late one night, along the empty street free of cars and people, free even of parked cars, the windows of the houses dark all around, unable to keep in the joy inside me in a closed environment, space, in the navy-blue suit, as I recall, with a red white and blue patriotic tie around my neck, uphill, up the steep incline, streetlamps shedding bright light through the dak green leaves of the trees onto the pavement, me, I casting a moving, forward-leaning shadow, must have been a little windy, the tie flapped around as I leaned forward, caressing my face like a silky, loving woman's hand, I charging up the hill practically running, joy, the joy of being, of being alive, strong, well dressed, like a car engine stuck in high gear roaring inside me, in the house, the big count's-palace house, a thin-stemmed wine glass with a big globe on top properly half-filled with red wine, dark, nearly black, slightly raspy like velvet barbed wire, but delicious, always red wine even if different brands, would go from room to room, turning on and off lights, admiring the art on the walls, order, emptiness of others, would put on a record, tape, listen, half-inclined on the leather sofa in the living room or the captain's bed in the little room upstairs where I had a tape player, a radio/tape-recorder/player, sipping the wine, on one of them a woman sang in a husky Marlene Dietrich voice a riff on "Only you," it was in another language, "Only you," she sang, "hot and hard," a slut, just like a man, well, not a slut like a man, men aren't sluts, something else, but bad in this respect just like a man, no, not bad, worse, men don't give birth, why aren't you all angels? who will we pray to if it's not you? a candle flickering on the windowsill next to my head on the right, no, not a candle, no candles, I never lit candles, not the type, a little lamp on the dresser discretely doing its job in the far right corner.

20

ONE MORE STEP, and I'm out in the open, in the *plazuela,* in the little square in front of the church, as always ready to make a beeline toward it, and at that instant see two women in a great hurry pass through the doorway and disappear inside it, there's something strange about it, tourists don't behave this way, don't move that fast, and local churchgoers don't either, it's as if the two had some business to do inside, something urgent and important, and they were walking too close together, seemed to be intimate with each other, too intimate for a couple of tourists or churchgoers, I just saw their backs, but there was something familiar about them, yes! of course! they were the ones, the first and the second! that's right, that's strange, that's really strange, that's amazing, upsetting, no wonder, no, it couldn't be! it couldn't be that they are together, that they are, that they have been all along in cahoots with each other against me, no! that's too awful, that's impossible! I'm all upset about it, boiling mad inside, have to make sure, have to be certain that that's what it is, and have to do something about it! I run, run fast, run like a sprinter, a champion sprinter that at one time I nearly was, get there in no time, make it through the door, there's no one to stop me, the church is empty, the two rows of pews are like dotted lines on a form, waiting to be filled in, I'm out of breath, walk slowly, looking around, casing the space, they're nowhere to be seen, I look in the chapel, it's empty too, where in hell could they be? they couldn't have disappeared, vanished into thin air, I'm not far from the confessional booth, it stands against the wall on the right just beyond the entrance to the chapel, hear some sounds coming from it, giggling or something like that, see the black curtain on it stir, there's someone inside, more than one person, moreover, yes, it's them, the two of them, they're making out with each other! God, that's incredible, that's unbelievable, that's unpardonable, the bitches! I have to do something about it, have to stop it, must punish them, I'll kill them! will kill them both! I'm ready to do it, but at that instant a flood of people coming in from the left bar my way, they are chattering and moving very fast, they are like water rushing in a river after a deluge or, better, like a river of mud in a landslide sliding along, I have to let them go by, otherwise I'll be swept along, they stream into the chapel, they're clearly tourists in a great hurry, if this is Tuesday, it must be Paris or the other way around or something like that, I wait impatiently, this goes on for a while, but finally it stops, all the people have gone into the chapel, my way is finally clear, the curtain on the confessional is pushed aside, the inside is empty, damn! the bitches have escaped! I turn my eyes left, there they are running down the empty aisle toward the altar, holding hands and skipping along like little girls playing a game, what bitches, I'll give it to them! I take off like a bullet and run after them, but they are moving fast too, they run past the altar to the left, there's a door there, they reach and open it, they jump through it as if into empty space, the door stays open, bright light streams in through it from below, as if in an airplane high up in the air, and I wake up, for some reason, Salamanca, for some reason Salamanca comes to my mind, Salamanca, golden city, city of yellow stone, burnt gold by the cruel Castilian sun, my face burning in the afternoon sunshine as I stood, trying not to stare into it, with the façade of the cathedral behind me, its portal spreading its arms wide in a gesture of protection and perhaps love for the photograph she, the first one took, the incredible blue Castilian sky overhead frightening like the stare of a madman, frightening also because of threatening to break up any moment into boulders which would rain down upon me and crush me as they did St Stephen in his painful martyrdom, no, remember now, not the cathedral, the old or the new one, the church of the Convento de San Esteban, the Convent of St Stephen, known for its façade, the famous façade, one of the finest examples of Plateresque, the forerunner, the father of the Hispanic, Latin American Churrigueresco, in the form of, the façade, the portal in the form of a reredos, an external reredos with St Stephen's martyrdom depicted in the tympanum high above, all beautifully, delicately, intricately carved, Plateresque, *Plateresco* refers to silversmithing, working in silver, with Spanish *plata* meaning silver, a golden city, Salamanca was, is, we, me and the first one, never went there with the second, the other loved it a lot and I didn't want to spoil it for her and at the same time myself, so me and the first one had been to Salamanca a number of times, three, four, don't remember exactly how many, but I think at least three or four, the first time stayed in a little hotel in the center of town where the elevator, the *ascensor* was operated by a boy maybe seven-eight years old, well, maybe nine or ten, he was small, but Spaniards were all small at the time, didn't consume enough protein and antibiotics, I towered over most of them, especially down south, at least half a head, and one day, this was in the morning, mid-morning, I asked him, the boy operating the elevator, why wasn't he in school, in the *colegio?* he went at night, he answered, God! a seven- or eight- or nine- or ten-year-old kid going to primary school at night! I went to graduate school at night, as everyone else did because that's when the classes were held as virtually all the students worked during the work hours, but I was four times older than he, the education, the education in Spain really bad at that time, many people I met were illiterate and few displayed great knowledge, provincial, antediluvial in general, the sister of a man I knew once was a doctor, studied at the University, the University of Salamanca, said she never saw a live patient, to remove an appendix they studied diagrams in an encyclopedia, not even a medical book, an encyclopedia! no wonder I was being treated for a stomach, gastric problem while suffering from colitis, a result of an E. coli infection that became chronic as I didn't attend to it for too long, saw an expert, a luminary, the best in Spain in the field, supposedly, García Garzón was his name, I think, or something like that , who happened to live in the town, *"Me duele el estómago,"* I said, as we would do in English, and he took it literally, I guess, I should have said *"Me duele la barriga,"* he never examined, touched me, asked to point where it hurt, describe the symptoms, God! the university, yes, that's what I was coming to, the man sharing the hand, the hand and gesture with the auxiliary priest Pedro Ruiz Durón, Antonio de Covarrubias, de Covarrubias y Leiva, El Greco's great friend, studied at the University of Salamanca, graduated from it with a degree in law in 1556, he was born in 1512, no, in 1514, I think, yes, in 1514, so he was 42 years old when he graduated, surprising, maybe he had a daytime job too and went to school at night, I didn't think they did such things back then, going to school at night, I mean, I'm joking, of course, he was apparently a late bloomer, bloomed very long, died in 1602 at the age of 88, very unusual for those times, anyway, so, two years after graduating he started teaching at the university, held the chair of Roman Civil Law, but in 1561 left for Granada and then to other places, and in 1580, after becoming a widower and partially deaf from some illness, came to Toledo, where he was born, was ordained a priest, served as the rector of St Catherine University, associated with the cathedral of Toledo that had been built by his architect father Alonso, became close friends with El Greco, and died there, died in 1602, enough, University of Salamanca, it's the oldest university in Spain and one of the oldest in the world, it was founded by King Alfonso IX of León in 1528, and has some illustrious graduates, which included, in addition to Antonio de Covarrubias and his older brother Diego, who attended the Third Council of Trent, with Antonio assisting him, whose face is depicted earlier in the painting, squeezed in between the Dominican and the Augustin monk, so, included such famous figures as Cervantes, Góngora, Calderon de la Barca, and Unamuno, and, yes, forgot, San Juan de la Cruz and Fray Luís de León, who became the rector and appears to be considered the most important one of all, there's a big statue of him in the courtyard, facing the entrance of the university, which, by the way, the entrance, I mean, looks very much like the entrance to the church of the St Stephen Convent, except with two small red doors instead of one big one and the

Yuriy Tarnawsky

façade, a likewise beautiful Plateresque façade, smaller and
not recessed, not looking like a reredos, there's also an
aula, a classroom named after him, with low coarse wooden
benches for sitting and similar tables in front of them for
writing on, there must have been a lot of back aching going
on there when they were used because there was nothing to
lean back on except the next table, and yes, the library, the
ceiling in the library, gently vaulted and painted blue with the
constellations upon it, both the stars and the creatures they
are supposed to represent, magnificent, amazing, similar
contemporary ones, like the huge one in the train station in
New York City without a doubt inspired by it, it, the university,
has a magnificent cloistered courtyard, with beautiful
unusual arches, I guess you might call them Plateresque,
Renaissance, transitional between Gothic and Baroque, a
magnificent city, Salamanca, loved it, especially the Plaza
Mayor, the eighth wonder of the world, smaller than the one
in Madrid but much more beautiful, the Madrid one severe,
the cruel, dour capital, imperial spirit, Salamanca science
and art, the square, the plaza, delicate, golden stone,
intricate carvings, and baroque arches, built in 1850, I think,
with an early retro look, picking up on the glorious bygone

past, we sat, I and the first one in one of the cafés in it one evening, out in the open, a quarrel ensued between two young bucks at a nearby table, university students, probably, even though it was in summer, during summer recess, maybe local ones, one of the two ripped off his shirt to show off his muscles, it looked like he did work out but wasn't that impressive, I was much more developed, I think, anyway, a show-off coward, tried to scare the other one, who looked weaker, but wasn't impressed, stayed cool, the others stepped in and things simmered down, they all behaved afterwards as if nothing had happened, easy, I mean, quickly come, quickly go, you could say, some people are like that, others hard as a rock, steel, me for instance, don't forget and don't forgive till the day they die.

21

FRANCISCO DE PISA, *el doctor* Francisco de Pisa, yes, the head with the piously heaven-raised eyes, sticking up between Antonio de Covarrubias and the auxiliary priest Pedro Ruiz Durón, as I suspected, is not just a gap fill-in, a visual expletive, but apparently that of Francisco de Pisa, a local historian who wrote extensively and, it is claimed, colorfully, about Toledo, in particular about the Santo Tomé church and the miracle of the burial of the Count of Orgaz, the heaven-raised eyes giving support to the hypothesis, although the visage, the facial features differ substantially from the portrait of the man El Greco painted around 1614, but that was almost thirty years later, between twenty-five and twenty-eight to be precise and only two years before his, Francisco de Pisa's death, so his appearance could have and would have changed significantly, compare for instance El Greco's 1600 portrait of an old man, which is generally considered to be a self-portrait, with his depiction of himself in the painting, in the painting of the burial of Orgaz, and besides, El Greco had little space to work with, little room for the portrait in the gap between Antonio de Covarrubias and Ruiz Durón to be painted, so the face, the visage had to be squeezed in, made narrow, elongated, which in addition fell within his, El Greco's, Mannerist style and esthetics, and in general, El Greco's depiction of people cannot be said to excel in realistic rendering, but rather in the effect it creates on the viewer, as is true of all Expressionist painters, which is what El Greco was, in case of multiple portraits of a person he painted, for instance, there are almost always significant differences in appearance, which must reflect El Greco's feeling about the model and intent, anyway, Francisco de Pisa, was born in 1534, four hundred years before me, well, closer to three hundred ninety-nine and a half, the last two digits of the year the same as mine but the month six higher, the day, let's see, nine, nine digits higher, so, to be really precise, he was born exactly three hundred ninety-nine years, six months, less nine days before me, born in Toledo, God, practically all of them were born in Toledo! still, the Spaniards have a saying, *Toledanas putas tempranas*, Toledan girls start whoring early, ha, ha! typical Spaniards,

Spanish men, hung up on virginity, *exclusivistas*, I heard one Spanish girl complain dejectedly, all the same, the girls are all the same everywhere, the same as men, procreation, continuation, transfer, survival of the genes, from amebae, one-cell organisms, to us, *homo sapiens, homo stultus,* all the same, anyway, enough, attended, Francisco de Pisa attended University of Salamanca, of course, they all did, first as a *criado* a servant, an orderly, I guess, a *Knabe für alles, un chico para todo*, a gofer, in other words, a gofer of the Covarrubias brothers Diego and Antonio, finished his studies at Santa Catalina University in Toledo, which was then under the direction of Antonio de Covarrubias, who was twenty years older than him, and got his doctor's degree in 1575 in Canonical Law, occupied various chairs at institutions of higher learning in Toledo and died there, died in 1616, as I mentioned, Pisa, Pisa, I thought Francisco was a foreigner who settled in Spain like El Greco, born in Italy, Pisa, but that was a family name, his father's family name, his parents were local people, apparently, parishioners of the San Román church, his father a doctor, Gonzalo de Pisa, and mother Elvira de Palma, anyway, Pisa, the city of Pisa, quite beautiful, actually, white, of white marble, white marble

Yuriy Tarnawsky

Salamanca, but no, I'm wrong, the city not beautiful and not of white marble, just the cathedral and the belltower of white marble and beautiful, the city nondescript, as I recall, shabby, known not for the beauty of its architecture, but for a blunder, a mistake in its most famous structure, the belltower, which leans ridiculously far out, I don't understand why it doesn't collapse, I did climb it, the belltower, I think, but refused to walk under it, afraid it'd fall down on me and crush me, visited, the city, Pisa, together with the first one, before Spain, I think, no, yes, before Spain, then that madwoman, the second one, pursued me there, couldn't be without me for a couple of weeks, the bitch, ruined my life, although the fault was mine, I didn't have enough spine to say, no, get lost! *verschwinde! verdufte!* paying for it now with Toledo, maybe not, probably not, probably not with Toledo, but have paid for it, paid dearly, like with paint under my finger nails and scratches on the walls in my bedroom while the dawn was pressing its pasty idiot's face from the outside against the windowpanes on all sides of the house, among others, paid with that for starters among others, anyway, enough, Pisa, the guilt, the agony I went through after she, the second one came! can't describe it, don't want

to describe it, describe what I did, too painful, too painful
and shameful, the drive, the two of us, the first one and me
did after the other one left, drive along the Italian Riviera,
along the narrow winding road dug into the sheer wall, the
almost vertical Ligurian coast, the sea on the left below, the
vast vague sea way down below that Rocco, my Rocco saw
through the seared, pale-fire grass through the space under
the tall black-topped umbrella pines, calling, the sea calling
out to those late for their funeral, calling them by their first
names, trying to reassure them, you're OK, OK, don't worry,
you're almost there, you're fine, one more turn, just one more
turn and you're there, you've arrived, you've made it!
stopped off in Genoa, rancid, sour lasagna for supper at the
sleazy pension right on the shore, the wharf, went swimming,
lukewarm water, ugh! two big turds, big fluffy turds bobbing
up and down next to my face, mouth, screamed, spat,
paddled like crazy back to the shore, the wharf, couldn't stop
taking showers and brushing my teeth all night, fancy
Europe, putting on airs now! the hole-in-the floor toilets
encrusted with shit of those days, eyes tearing from
ammonia in the pissoirs, the stink of sweat and garlic in the
crowded Paris Metro cars during the morning rush hours

when I was going to work, Paris, oh, yes, this was at Odile's place, when I got sick, sick with the trots, the European trots of those times, and she called that doctor, she knew, they still did house calls in those days, and he praised my looks when he came and saw me in bed, miserable and with tousled hair, looking like Rimbaud in the hotel room in Brussels after being shot by Verlaine, which made me feel proud and better.

22

PEDRO RUIZ DURÓN, the auxiliary priest, who is also called sometimes the bursar of the Santo Tomé church or its trustee, stands with his back turned to the viewer, eyes raised to heaven, some commentators describing the stance as a sign of his turning his back on the funeral and putting his faith in afterlife, in other words, a sign of his showing scorn for the flesh, which, being material, is perishable and destined to die, and extolling the soul, which, being spiritual, is immortal and assured of eternal life at Christ's side in heaven, which may be true, that is, there is no denying that it is possible to interpret the priest's stance as a sign of what was said and also reasonable to assume El Greco was aware of such a possibility and even likely that this was one of the reasons why he painted the man as he did, but if so, it was almost certainly not the only reason and just as certainly not the primary one why he acted this way, El Greco was first and foremost a painter and his goal was to paint as perfect a picture as possible, there are twenty six figures in the row of stokers in the painting, and having all of them face the viewer may have been acceptable, but it would not have been interesting, rather, it would have looked standard, predictable, even boring, but, with Ruiz Durón's back turned to the viewer, we have an unusual, visually interesting composition, note that he, the priest, that is, his torso and the reach-out of his arms, takes up practically half of the painting, of the row of stokers, from the sixteenth figure, the proto-Existentialist with the dejected face to the twenty-sixth one, the head with the weird glass eye directed skyward, with this, El Greco gets the added opportunity of lending the priest's left hand to Antonio de Covarrubias to make his gesture and a double response, that of Covarrubias and the priest, to the right hand gesture of the eighteenth figure, and the priest's right hand, its gesture, now in addition serves as the necessary counterpoint to the first hand gesture of the six in the painting, that of the black-habited Augustine monk on the very left, so, by doing what he did, El Greco has introduced a refreshing variety into the painting and solved the problem with the hand gesture motif, which adds richness to the painting by providing its final element, without which the design would have looked incomplete, Ruiz Durón also provides El Greco with the opportunity to show off his skill in rendering texture, the surplice, the long, long-sleeved white shirt the priest is wearing is shown to be of thin, sheer gossamer material, through which the black cassock is shining through, he, El Greco achieves this by painting it different shades of gray, or rather, pure white and different shades of gray, ranging from near-white to near-black, representing the thickness of the fabric and its closeness to the black undergarment, the white indicating the fabric is folded or creased and the gray that it is in a single layer hanging loose or pressed respectively farther from or closer to the cassock, the effect is quite good, although not outstanding, I seem to feel that I have seen technically more skillful representations of this, not sure whose or where, in Botticelli's *Primavera,* perhaps, with the seductive naked bodies of the three graces and the nymph Chloris showing through their white gossamer dresses, but perhaps even better by others, although I can't pinpoint by whom, and also in sculpture, that is, I have a feeling that I have seen a more skilled rendering of fabric in sculpture, such as the cloth draped over Christ's lap in

DaVinci's *Pietà,* and come to think of it, even more in Mary's dress, and also by others, even going as far back as ancient Greek sculpture, by Phidias, perhaps, or others, but I don't think El Greco should be criticized for this, he was, after all, an Expressionist, striving for effect rather than realistic representation, and the effect of what he has done is excellent, partly probably because the quality of his painting is without doubt very good, but partly, I suspect, because it contrasts with the stark, simplified Expressionist technique of most of the painting, it is possible, for instance, that the reason the rendering of the super sheer gossamer fabric in *Primavera* may seem better is the fact that the viewer sees the delicate feminine forms shining through it, whereas in El Greco's painting we have only plain black cloth, anyway, right and left, yes, the beach was divided into two parts, la Primera Playa and la Segunda, the First Beach and the Second, the First on the right and the Second on the left, looking out to the sea, which were separated by a rocky outcrop, promontory, with a beautiful little park, or gardens, as it was called, on top, with white-painted railings along the edges, for visitors' protection, and likewise white benches along them facing out, with comfortable curved backs for people to sit in and enjoy the breath-taking vistas, their chests nesting places for white swans to come flying in, while listening to Heitor Villa-Lobos' *Bachianas Brazileiras No. V* being sung by an angelic disembodied female voice, the two, the two beaches, looked like the wings of a supergiant bird, spread out wide, flying in toward the land, with the outcrop, the promontory, its head, the left wing, that is, the one on the right, shorter and more straight, and the right one, that is, the one on the left, longer and more curving, the disparity between the two, however, not marring the image, not making the bird seem crippled, deformed, but appearing to be due to the position from which the viewer was seeing it, so, the First Beach was shorter and nearly straight, rocks, a lot of rocks, some of them big, on which *percebes*, goose barnacles, grew and were harvested, on its right end, near the Guardia Civil *cuartel,* barracks, beyond which lay the peninsula on which stood the royal summer palace which was used at the time as one of the venues for the International Summer University, the two parts were usually separated at the promontory by the sea, by water, and you could walk uninterrupted along it only when the tide was out, I liked, preferred to run along it then, for it would be less boring, less monotonous, I wouldn't have to repeat turning around so many times, the right part, as I recall, was about a quarter of a mile long, and the left one about twice that, or about half a mile, so, if I were to do my usual eight-mile workout, which at the easy pace of eight miles per hour would take an hour, I'd have to do sixteen laps on the right short one, which was a drag, and eight on the long me, which was better, but still a bit boring, but with the tide out, with the full beach, which would be about three quarters of a mile long, I'd cover the distance in a little over five laps, I don't remember now if I did this, but knowing myself, I probably did five and a half laps and walked the return half, cooling off, making sure I had covered the full eight miles, afraid I may have overestimated the distances, which I probably did, you never saw anyone running in those days, people would laugh and point fingers at me as I ran in the morning in the streets, sometimes I'd hear them call out, *Mira, mira, mira!* provoking laughter, provincial bumpkins, cut off from the rest of the world! but not on the beach, not when I ran on the beach, there, they just ignored me, strange, I guess it was the context, the environment, somehow it made a difference, but I never saw anyone else run on the beach, not, except once a young jerk decided to compete with me, it was on the First Beach, the Primera Playa, on which I ran when it was more convenient for me and I didn't want to wait till the tide was out, he saw me running and decided he should prove to me and himself, and probably especially to everyone who saw us that he was better, stronger, more *macho* than me, I'd been running for a while and then, as I was starting a new lap, I saw a guy about fifty yards away running toward me, I checked later and sure enough, he was following me, he ran faster than me, gradually catching up, so I sped up a little, at the next turn-around he was a little closer, but not that much, so I speeded up some more, sure he wouldn't catch me, but then, as I was approaching the turn-around, I heard him breathing heavily right behind me, he sprinted past me, made it to the rock some ten yards away and stopped, he'd made it! he beat me! a stupid jerk, like the one in Salamanca, who took off his shirt, trying to start a fight, I ran another ten laps or however many there were left at my pace, anyway, boys and young men would play paddle ball by the promontory on the First Beach, where that guy had stopped, using a tennis ball and big flat paddles, quite a bit bigger and with a longer handle than those used in ping-pong, one standing with his back to the rock, and the other one some twenty-thirty feet away, facing him, slamming the ball as hard as he could, directing it at his partner, who was supposed to hit it back, which he almost invariably did, they usually did this for a long time, I don't know, twenty-thirty rallies at a time or more, sometime much more, maybe a few hundred, it must have gone on for minutes sometimes, five-ten, no, not ten, maybe six seven, or just five-six, five-six minutes, anyway, for a long time, I admired them, couldn't have done it myself, wished I could try it, but never dared to ask, too bashful, timid, they were all friends and younger than me too, some almost ten years younger, those in their teens, anyway, I was unable to stop thinking about them, wanted to be there, one of them, hitting the ball, hearing the sound it made hitting the flat wooden surface on and on, as I lay stretched out on my towel reading one of the books I brought along to Spain to read, Spinoza, or Heidegger, or Jaspers, or Unamuno's *Del sentimiento trágico de la vida, On the Tragic Sense of Life,* which I'd bought in town.

23

THE MAN DIRECTLY to the right of the auxiliary priest Pedro Ruiz Durón, that is, directly on his right hand side, looks amazingly similar to the one four spaces, that is, four figures to the left, the one directly to the right of the third knight of Santiago, the proto-Existentialist figure with the dejected face, who, the fourth man to the left, extends his right hand toward the left one of the priest, which, together with the priest's, form a two-hand composition, a matching pair to that formed by the two hands of the first knight of Santiago, the supposed mayor of Toledo, the figure directly to the right of El Greco, the two men, that is, the man on the right of the priest and the fourth one to the left, look like brothers, perhaps twins, identical twins, although the man on the right of the priest appears to be somewhat older, not much, a few years perhaps, but still older, his left hand is shown clutching the staff of the tall cross with the elaborate crucifix on top that reaches almost to heaven, to the upper part of the painting, which seems to imply that he is somehow connected to the church, to Santo Tomé, and this seems to be further suggested by his closeness to the priest, the same seems to be true of his probable brother, the man four spaces to the left, since his hand almost touches that of the priest, he appears to be a figure of some stature, apparently more important than his probable brother, who perhaps may be just a minor official in the parish, a priest, as suggested by what can be seen of his clothing, since he, the man four spaces to the left, occupies a place so close to the center of the painting, is depicted in greater detail, and is more lavishly dressed, the suggestion that the two brothers, if this is what they are, are both linked in some way to the Santo Tomé church may seem to be an overreach, but actually is not at all surprising, families in those days were frequently patrons of particular churches, perhaps because of an event, a miracle of some sort or something similar that was attributed to the patron saint of that church, which took place in the past in the family's history, so this is probably what we are dealing with here, there was a second, that is another, but much smaller beach in town, named after the peninsula with the former royal summer palace on it that was used as one of the buildings of the International Summer University, it was a little triangular area, tucked into the space between the neck of the peninsula and its wide body, and was sheltered by the topography of the coast and the peninsula, it was located not on the open sea, but on the inlet into the bay, along which the city stretched, seen from the high promenade that ran along the bay into town, it looked like a shelter, in which the beachgoers, mostly the International Summer University students sunning themselves after classes, had gathered apparently for the purpose of protection, hiding from something unwanted, opposite it, across the inlet, lay the biggest and the most beautiful beach in town, although it wasn't strictly speaking in town, since the land on that side of the inlet and along the bay all the way to its head didn't belong to the city but to a number of *comarcas*, villages or towns that stretched alongside it, and to get to it you had to take a ferry or drive some thirty or forty kilometers along the coast, the beach was a long, curved, sandy spit that was nearly flooded at high tide and cut off from the coast and it was dangerous to get caught on it because of the *resaca,* the undertow, which would drag you into the inlet and carry you out to sea, I, I mean, we, the two of us, the first one and me, went out there only once, taking the ferry, which was just a small boat capable of carrying perhaps half a dozen people, and which you hired at your own risk, relying on the honesty of the owner or the pilot who operated the boat to come and get you out in time, in our case there were only the two of us there, in the boat and on the beach, as the few people that had been there when we arrived, had been picked up earlier by other boats, apparently private ones, so, in our case, the man was late and we watched with alarm as the water keep rising and the beach kept shrinking, and at one point packed our things and moved close to where the spit joined the land to make sure we could get out in time, but just then a boat come out of the marina across the bay and headed toward us, it was the ferry, it picked us up, and as we expressed our gratitude to the man for coming, he replied with some indignation in his voice that he had never left anyone stranded there in the many years, whatever it was, ten or something, that he'd been in business, and that it was against the law to do that, and that, anyway, it was his word and that it was stronger than the law, a typical Spaniard, a hidalgo, meaning *hijo de algo*, son of something, of whom there were almost as many as *hjos de nada*, sons of nothing, each poorer than the next one, like the one from a nameless place in la Mancha, with *lanza en astillero, adarga antigua, rocín flaco y galgo corredor,* whose expenses on his meager daily diet consumed three quarters of his income, at night, in the moonlight, the bay looked like a giant apple orchard in bloom and you couldn't tear your eyes away from the sight as you walked along the promenade, we would stop there and stand for a long time, leaning on the railing, not moving and not saying a word, before proceeding home, the street turned left at the entrance to the peninsula, where the Guardia Civil barracks stood, and proceed along the open coast, now framed on both sides by the short gnarled tamarisk trees, turned for brief stretches into bowers, as if for newlyweds to walk through, I would ran along it when I wasn't running on the beach, sometimes dipping into the peninsula when I ran on the way to town, that provided a brief relief, change in scenery, but it wasn't that long, half a mile at the most, then about three quarters of a mile into town, turn around, would usually skip the peninsula this time, then along the coast again, past the First and the Second Beach, past the football, that is *fútbol,* or soccer, stadium, up the highway framed by the big plane trees, to the *Faro*, the lighthouse, that stands there on the edge of the high bluffs, overlooking the sea, where I once willed my ashes to be thrown into the air, so that they'd flutter like a gray flag for a few seconds over the desolate waters, after my body was burned like a hated or forbidden book, and retrace may way back home, turning right at the big café and running along the wide street with the grounds of the little palace that stood there on my left to the apartment building at the end.

24

NO, NO, I was wrong, I've been wrong all along, the man, the face behind the staff of the cross held by the man directly to the right of the auxiliary priest Pedro Ruiz Durón, the one who looks like the older brother of the man directly to the right of the third knight of Santiago, in spite of being barely visible, of being depicted so sketchily, is not a fill-in, as I have been suggesting, assuming, none of them are, I mean, none of the figures depicted in the painting, no matter how sketchily they be represented, are mere fill-ins, but are real, actual people, people, El Greco knew and felt obliged for one reason or another to put in the painting, I am sure of that, how could it be otherwise? he was a great artist and in this painting wanted to pay homage to the memory of the Lord, the Count of Orgaz by the strongest means possible, which must include having in the painting as many individuals as would fit in, so why would he waste precious space on some meaningless, carelessly done daubing? no, never, of that I'm sure, so, the figure, the face hiding behind the staff held by the hand of the man directly to the right of the auxiliary priest Pedro Ruiz Durón must represent, or with great likelihood represents a real person, one likely of little importance, little stature, but someone, who El Greco thought deserved or at the least was acceptable to be depicted in the painting, in the case of this particular individual, probably some very minor official in the hierarchy of the Santo Tomé parish, church, the same then must be said about, how many are there of these? let's see, one, two three, four, five, so, the same must be said of five additional figures, faces in the painting, going from left to right, first, the one on the right of the black-habited Augustin monk, the one directly under the third torch flame, and the four heads piled up helter-skelter above the figures represented fully to the right of the center of the painting, for a total, with the man hiding behind the staff of the cross held by the man directly to the right of the auxiliary priest Pedro Ruiz Durón, of six, a total of six figures of less importance than the rest of the men in the row of stokers, six, yes, six, the apartment consisted of three bedrooms, the master bedroom and my and her studies, mine bigger than hers, which she liked, as it went better, in her words, with her more lyrical personality, a living room, a connected dining room, and the kitchen, it had also a hallway, two bathrooms, and two balconies, one up front, facing the sea, and one in the back, facing the yard, the front balcony was accessible from my study and from the living room, and we would frequently have breakfast there, sitting in the low, comfortable wicker chairs, with a matching low glass-topped wicker coffee table before us, usually tea with honey and lemon and some pastry, I'd pick up at a nearby *tienda,* like *palmeras, bizcochos*, or croissants, that is, *curas sanos,* healthy priests, as they were sometimes called, with the bitterness of the widespread anticlericalism turned into humor, there was a narrow single bed against the wall in my study in the local traditional style, custom made as all the furniture in the apartment with the exception of the kitchen, on which I would take occasional pit-stop naps, including those of the siesta, and a likewise narrow table in the center with a chair next to it, sitting at it, by turning my head left, I could see through the glass door leading onto the balcony a thin strip of the sea protruding above the flat roof of the big café that stretched along good part of the beach, the Primera Playa, that lay directly under it, her room, study was much smaller, it was intended for a maid, and with its single narrow window looked like a cell, not a prison cell but one in a convent, which was appropriate and which could have been part of the reason she liked it because in one of her frantic early forays into finding herself she converted to Catholicism, from Protestantism to Catholicism, and planned to become a nun, a Poor Clare no less, until she slipped on her sex and wound up rolled into a ball at my feet, a bed and a chair like mine and a beautifully sculptured tall secretary constituted all of the furniture in the room, a big double bed, *cama de matrimonio*, or marriage bed, the kind, El Gallo, the bullfighter Rafael Gómez Ortega, the elder brother of the great Joselito, El Gallito, had in mind when he described the *cuna*, or cradle, that is, the spread of the horns of a giant bull he once had to fight, so, a big double bed with a tall elaborate headboard, two night tables at its sides, a chest of drawers, and a chair to sit on as you were getting dressed or undressed took up all the space of the bedroom, as the other two rooms, it had a built-in wardrobe, its glass door opened onto the other balcony, which was narrow and ran the width of the apartment and was also accessed through the glass door in the kitchen, the room was dark because it was shaded by the balcony on the floor above and also because the backyard onto which it looked out had a few tall palm trees growing in it which made it dark, there was a parrot, a *loro,* living in a cage in the yard, don't remember where exactly, but most certainly not on one of the palms trees, it would have been too high, probably on the wall or off the eave, off the overhang of the big garage that stood in the back, it, the parrot came from some nearby village and had been given to someone living in the building because it had picked up a bad habit of calling out the vulgar name for the female sex organ, *coño,* all the time, which it must have heard a lot as it was growing up, it polluted the speech and minds of the kids in the neighborhood, you heard the word echoing all day in the yard, enounced in a loud crystalline voice, it went on for a while, a few months perhaps, but then one day it, the parrot was gone, it must have been returned to its previous owner, given away to some unsuspecting innocent, or served in an *arroz con loro* dish, to unsuspecting family members or guests, a big mirror in an ornate golden frame, especially chosen to go with the stark furniture, hung on the wall in the dining room above a long cabinet with cuarterones, which housed an eight-place baroque blue-on-white *vajilla,* dinnerware set made to order in Talavera de la Reina, where Joselito, El Gallito, was killed by that Fred Astaire of a bull Bailador, plus silverware, tablecloths, napkins, and other things like that, a long table, the length of the cabinet, and eight chairs with leather seats and backs, six regular ones, three on each side, and two *sillones,* big ones, with arm rests, at the ends, stood alongside it, with a solid brass chandelier hanging down from the ceiling above, an exact copy of the one that hangs in the bedroom, the alcove, where Felipe II, the King Philip II, spent his last days in the El Escorial Palace, or rather, Monastery, with a window next to the bed overlooking the altar so that he could hear the mass being said in the church below every morning, noon, and night, and against the opposite wall, a *vargueño,* stood a *vargueño* with a beautifully carved front containing two lions facing each other across a square cross, that served as a bar, holding bottles of wine and liquor and glasses instead of the intended starched linens, the door onto the front balcony was on the left, at the end of the cabinet, separating the dining room from the living room, a wicker sofa with a glass-topped wicker coffee table and two armchairs in the style of the furniture on the balcony, but with canvas cushions on the sofa and armchairs, stood, facing the single huge glass-plate window which took up all of the wall, through which, looking straight out as you stood or sat on the sofa or one of the armchairs, you could see the same thin strip of the sea protruding above the flat roof of the big café as from my study, all rooms were accessed from the hallway, the first door on the right into the dining room, that is the dining-living room, the one on the left into the kitchen, the next two on the right into our bathrooms, first mine, with a toilet, sink, and shower stall, its walls covered with small, square glazed brown tiles, perhaps two centimeters on the side that looked like square bubbles, hers similar to mine but bigger, with a bathtub and a shower over it, its walls covered with the same kind of tiles except aquamarine in color, the floors in both bathrooms were of white marble, the next door on the left led to the master bedroom, the one on the right directly across from it into my study, and the door straight ahead into hers, a wide street led from the apartment building to the sea, to the café at its end, about two hundred meters long, shaded on both sides by big old plane trees, it wasn't called *avenida,* avenue, however, but *calle,* street, a sizeable property behind an iron fence, with tall umbrella pines in the back and a beautiful little palace at the end, its windows always shuttered, but not looking abandoned, called Palacio de los Pinares, or Pine Trees Palace, stretched along the right side of the street all the way to the sea, that is to the street that ran along the coast and past the café, when you came to it, to the end of the street, the wide street, you could turn right and walk into town, past the Guardia Civil barracks and the entrance to the peninsula and then along the bay, or left, along the café, past the promontory gardens, along the Second Beach, past the soccer stadium, and up the road on to the *Faro*, the lighthouse, the address, the street number of the apartment building was twenty-four, I think, was it? or twenty-six? not sure, not quite sure, no, no, remember now, not twenty-four, it ended in a six, six, yes, so, either sixteen or twenty-six, thirty-six would be too high, the street wasn't that long, on second thought, twenty-six would be probably too high too, so, sixteen, yes, it must have been sixteen, sixteen for sure, no, not for sure, twenty-six, for sure, remember now distinctly, twenty-six, yes, but so what? what does it matter? who gives a damn? who would be looking for the place now?

25

THE NEXT TO the last figure on the right in the row of stockers, the man who is reading in a book and is wearing a richly embroidered cape over his black soutane or whatever it is that he has underneath, is the Santo Tomé parish priest Andrés Núñez de Madrid, at whose initiative, on March 18, 1586, El Greco signed the contract to do the painting, but he, Andrés Núñez, was the driving force behind the project and did much more than that, first, Don Gonzalo Ruiz de Toledo, at that time the Señor or Lord of the town of Orgaz because the family didn't rise to the rank of countship until 1522, committed in his will the town, upon his death, to pay to the Santo Tomé church each year a tribute of goods and money amounting to 2 sheep, 16 hens, 2 skins of wine, 2 wagon loads of firewood, and 800 coins *maravedis,* whatever that is, but, after dutifully carrying out its obligation for a number of years, at one point, the town decided to renege on the promise, apparently feeling it could get away with it, in 1564, however, Andrés Núñez, on his own initiative, brought a lawsuit against the town and, against all odds, won the case five years later, in 1569, at the Chancery of Valladolid, the settlement included the arrears, and the church, very modest until then, suddenly became quite wealthy, so that it was ultimately able to hire a top artist such as El Greco to do the painting, next, the idea of honoring Don Gonzalo Ruiz with a painting was purely that of Andrés Núñez, since there was no such stipulation in the will, but for him to proceed with his plan, first, the reburial of the count, which took place in 1327, or four years after his death in 1323, had to be recognized as a miracle, and second, an official permission of the church had to be obtained for the painting to be done and installed in the church, both of which Andrés Núñez, unstoppable that he was, achieved in 1583, so without him, without Andrés Núñez, the same as without El Greco, there wouldn't be a painting, commemorating the reburial of Don Gonzalo Ruiz de Toledo in the Santo Tomé church, well, actually no, actually not true, without El Greco there wouldn't be the painting we have in the Santo Tomé church now, but with Andrés Núñez, there, we certainly would have one, a different one, for sure, perhaps not as great, but there certainly would have been a painting in the Santo Tomé church that commemorated the reburial of the Count of Orgaz, so, in some sense, Andrés Núñez' contribution to it, to the existence of the painting is greater than that of El Greco, not on the artistic level, of course, but on the level of its existence, but wait, wait, I forgot, even more, there's even more to the whole thing, the contract El Greco signed on March 18, 1586, was not a simple contract, stating that a painting had to be delivered, but one that specified in some detail how the painting was to look, that it was to have a terrestrial and a heavenly part, that the body of the count was to be shown being lowered into the grave, that the two saints were to be there doing it, and even how each was supposed to hold the count, St Steven by the legs and St Augustin by the shoulders, and finally that a row of notables was supposed to be witnessing the event, in other words, a detailed design of the painting that El Greco merely had to adhere to, so, Andrés Núñez made a contribution to the painting also on the artistic level, and it is not insignificant to boot! given this, it is strange that he is given so little credit, I mean that his depiction in the painting is given so little importance, it is relatively small and appears in the very corner of the painting, being actually the last one fully represented figure in the row of stokers, really strange! by contrast, the auxiliary priest Pedro Ruiz Durón is shown closer to the center and is allotted a huge amount of space, with the span of his arms, he occupies at least a quarter of the width of the painting, far more than anyone else, so this is strange and is not insignificant, a great artist doesn't leave anything to chance, everything he does has a significance, there was apparently a dispute between El Greco and Andrés Núñez as to the value of the painting after it had been completed, some experts, two, as I recall, evaluated it as being worth 1,200 ducats, this was apparently an enormous sum, and, devoted as he was to Santo Tomé and sensitive to the issue of money, Andrés Núñez was shocked by it and tried to negotiate the figure down, which El Greco obviously didn't like, a second evaluation was conducted, but it actually turned out to be much higher, 1,600 ducats, no less, which was apparently completely unreasonable, and so the two settled for the original sum of 1,200 ducats, now, El Greco is said to have been a difficult and combative person, and it's possible and even likely that he bore a grudge against the priest and paid him back by diminishing his role in the

painting, I don' know what the auxiliary priest Pedro Ruiz
Durón, who is sometimes referred to as the steward or the
bursar of the church, played in this dispute, but it is possible
that he was on El Greco's side and the latter elevated him in
the painting over Andrés Núñez as a reward, but on second
thought, perhaps no, perhaps not, in spite of being squeezed
in the horizontal dimension in the painting, Andrés Núñez is
actually given quite a bit of vertical space, his beautiful cape
hangs way down below Pedro Ruiz Durón's modest shirt, or
chasuble, or whatever you call the thing that he's wearing,
so I may be wrong on this, anyway, it's not important, not
that important, I think, I'm making too much of it, both priests
are in the painting and that's what counts, enough, the sea,
the sea, can't get it out of my mind, the sea sometimes
seemed to be glued carelessly onto the horizon like a strip
of blue paper, sticking away at the bottom so that you could
see under it seaweed, fishes, rocks, and so on, like garbage
it was meant to cover up, the bare feet of the sand would be
seen then scurrying away like crazy in the direction where
there was more water, people, like pins with black round
heads were stuck into it here and there and stood still,
incapable of moving, on its edge, way in the distance, a wave

would break from time to time with a loud snapping sound like a long, thin piece of glass you twisted in your fingers, children would gather at the rock, the promontory, dividing the beach like foam, lining up their wide-open mouths in a straight line, forming one giant smile, and all around blue boats were swimming, covered with fish scales instead of having oars, when you saw black smoke rising from the smokestacks of a ship way in the distance, it meant that a person was dying somewhere at that instant, I once swam there in December, December 10 to be exact, it was on the Second Beach, unusual, unusual, but not unheard-of, it was warm, pretty warm, like a cool summer day, sunshine, warm sunshine, the water actually warmer, relatively warmer than the air, not much colder than in the summer, the warm current, that's what makes the climate there so mild, was alone, the second one was gone and the first one didn't want to come, sat up on the towel after drying myself off, supporting myself in the back with both arms, slender, slender like the columns in a Romanesque cloister, all of me like a Romanesque cloister with no one in it.

26

THE LAST MAN on the right in the row of stokers, the
companion of the fifteenth figure, who stands with his left
shoulder turned to the viewer and is leaning his head way
back, looking up the birth canal, watching the count's soul
being delivered, being born, so the last man in the row of
stokes, the one likewise positioned awkwardly, who's also
staring up to heaven with his fixed, glass-like eye, must
belong to the Santo Tomé church too, it looks like all five
figures, starting with the auxiliary priest or bursar of the
church Pedro Ruiz and going all the way to the right do, in
other words, first him, that is, Pedro Ruiz Durón, then the
man holding the tall cross, next the one whose face is hidden
behind the staff of the cross, after that the parish priest
Andrés Núñez de Madrid, and finally the man at the end,
who's looking up to heaven, they all must be connected to
the Santo Tomé church, he, the last man in the row, wears
something white draped over the black coat or whatever it

may be that he has on, which actually looks like something with a white-edged collar sticking up similarly to what the two priests are wearing under their outward garb, so he, the last man in the row, may be a priest too, one of a lower rank perhaps, a deacon, for instance, yes, for sure, almost for sure, El Greco starts mostly with church people, the two monks, on the left and ends with them, that is, with church people, on the right, while packing the space in-between with all sorts of lay luminaries, cultural figures, scholars, government officials, the supposed mayor of Toledo, for instance, and other members of the Spanish, Castilian high *hidalguía,* nobility, aristocracy, a wise man, a man with good business acumen, looking out for himself, with profit always on his mind, as some Greeks seem to be, nothing wrong with that, I wish I had some, had more of it, anyway, I've been calling the man, the last man on the right in the row of stokers, positioned awkwardly and having a glass eye, wrong, he is cramped in the tight space he's been allotted and stands as best he can, stands perfectly normally, straight, given where he is, he must crane his neck and look up toward heaven, for where else can he look? if he looked down, he'd be looking at his feet somewhere in the darkness before him, and from where he stands there's no way he could see the tomb, so he can't be shown trying to do that, so, the sky, heaven, is the only place he can look up to, and his eye isn't so strange, actually, it's pronounced, exaggerated, it's true, but El Greco had to make sure, the viewer, the viewer of the picture realizes the man is looking up, skyward, toward heaven, specifically at Christ, so he had to paint the eye with clarity, emphasis, realism wouldn't have worked here, exaggeration would and does, always does, as is the case with Expressionism, and after all, he was essentially an Expressionist, he does something similar with one of the heads, the third one from the left out of the four piled up helter-skelter above and just to the right of the center of the row of stokers, the position of the head of that man is similar to that of the last one on the right, except a bit more exaggerated, a clear companion to the other man's head, anyway, early evenings, that is, late afternoons, after 6PM, we'd stroll down the broad avenue, that is, the broad street toward the sea, the big café, sit at one of the tables outside near the balustrade overlooking the beach, the First Beach, it'd be vermouth with soda, or *manzanilla, manzanilla Jerez*, that is, or *oloroso dulce*, or *una cervezita,* or *un café* for her and *un té*, this time *un té de manzanilla*, for me, or toward the end more frequently *churros con chocolate, buen espesa, buen espesita, la chocolate,* the color of her eyes faded, gone, feet no longer dreaming of sky-blue cats and milk-chocolate-brown suede but of vast planes with lines of perspective vanishing on the horizon drawn on them, littered with dust balls, crumpled love letters, and dirty underwear, she'd been disappearing during the afternoons at the time and one day I decided to follow her, she walked, so I thought I'd take the bus, the electric trolleybus that ran to town, I waited a few minutes, went out, and caught it soon afterwards, about a half a mile down the road, I saw her walking quickly along the promenade, the bay on her left, once in town, I hid behind a corner of a building and waited for her to come, it wasn't certain she wouldn't have turned off earlier, but after about a quarter of an hour or so I saw her walking briskly as earlier, I let her pass and followed discreetly at some distance behind her, she cut through the park in the center of town and headed for the cluttered old part on the little hill behind it, aha, I thought, soon she'll be screwing with someone in a big messy bed in one of those cramped, dark bedrooms up there! with my heart in my throat, I followed her, hugging walls and ducking into doorways from time to time, but she walked on and on without slowing down, eventually, she wound up in the little plaza in front of the old cathedral, a tryst, I thought, she's meeting him in the church, the perverted bitch! she paused for an instant, got a kerchief out of her handbag, put it on, and disappeared in the dark open door, my heart still in my throat and beating more loudly than ever, I rushed forward, ran up the steps, and as she'd done, went through the dark door inside, afraid of being seen, I halted by the door post or whatever you call it, it was out of stone, of course, not wood, so, I stopped in the door, hugging its side and looked around, it was dark, and I couldn't see much at first, just the outlines of some people, half a dozen or so, huddling/ hiding in the pews, I sat in one of them in the back and eventually spotted her in one of them up front, near the altar, sitting still, her head bent forward, then she kneeled down on the stoop and stayed still, with her hands clutched together, elbows resting on the back of the pew before her, she was praying, of course, I was surprised because I converted her to atheism, Existentialism, Sartre's atheistic Existentialism, not Jacques Maritain's, after we got together, thought it was for good, but it obviously wasn't, it upset me, upset me almost as much as if I'd caught her in bed with another man, betrayal! I felt betrayed, then she put her hands on the edge of the back of the pew in front of her and pressed her head, her forehead to it and started hitting it on the back of the pew, not strongly, but clearly doing that, I was overcome with grief, shame, the pain was overwhelming, I couldn't bear the sight, wanted to run away but couldn't, that wouldn't change anything, the fact, but why? I asked, I got rid of the other one, finally got rid of the leach that'd latched onto me and was sucking my blood and my life, so why? it was unbearable because I couldn't change it, couldn't change the past, you can't change the past, it's part of you like your body, which you can't escape, in the meantime, she'd stopped what she'd been doing and was just sitting there, thinking, meditating, I think, not praying, but after a while she began to fidget, stir, clearly getting ready to leave, what'll I do? I thought, she'll see me, the confessional was just a few steps away, I thought of hiding in it, but then realized she might see me doing it, she might get up at exactly that time, besides maybe she planned to go to confession and

I'd have to pretend to be the priest, a Spanish priest with my slight but undeniable foreign accent, no way, an idiotic idea, duck into the pew? crouch there? not much better, wouldn't she be intrigued by the sight of someone hiding in the pew? she mercifully set me free from the predicament on her own, she got up and headed for the door, I froze, sat down a little on the bench, bent my head forward, tucked in the chin, she walked past where I sat, thank God, on the far side of the pews, and walked out, I waited a long time before leaving the church to make sure she'd be gone, took the bus, the trolleybus home, she wasn't back when I got there, came about half an hour later, had bought some fruit, *duraznos*, as I recall, sort of a small, flattened peach, quite tasty, so, she said she stopped by at the market and picked up some *duraznos*, added, the walk had done her good, it's the twenty-sixth today I think, saw it somewhere in town, must be January or February, not March, I think, no, not March, it's too cold and gets dark too early at night for March, and not December either, couldn't be the boxing day, the day after Christmas, there'd be too much going on, too much hullabaloo, like there would have been yesterday and the day before yesterday, I think we had it already, I mean, Christmas and the hullaballoo, I sort of remember, lights, and music, and singing in the streets, *Pero mira cómo beben los peces en el río*, and *La virgen se está peinando*, and the smell of *mazapanes* and *turrones* everywhere, no, not February, December would feel much farther away, January, probably, yes, it must be January 26, it is for sure.

27

THE MAN, THAT is, the youth, the person who's holding up
the legs of the Count of Orgaz is St Stephen, the counterpart
of St Augustin, who's holding him, holding the body up by
the shoulders or the back, it isn't clear which because the
saint's hands are not shown, being hidden by his huge,
loose, robe and the body of the count, the reason why the
two saints are there is, of course, because they participated
in the miracle, but the reason they did that was because way
back in 1312, or eleven years before the count's death and
fifteen before the miracle, some Augustine monks who
resided at the compound of the church of St Stephen
someplace on the banks of the Tajo, the river Tagus, outside
the city walls, had to leave the place because it became
unhealthy to live in, probably because of being situated in
the valley and close to water, and thanks to the count's
intervention had moved to some houses and the royal palace
owned by Queen María de Molina, the wife of king Sancho

the Brave, and furthermore, the new church that was to be built with the count's money was to be named after St Stephen, the same as the old one, he, St Stephen, is shown to be very young, by the looks of it, a teenager, the second youngest person in the picture, in the terrestrial part of the picture, outyouthed, so to speak, only by El Greco's son Jorge Manuel on his right below, he, St Stephen is also dressed in a voluminous robe that is way too big for him, this probably for compositional reasons, in order to counteract adequately St Augustin's big one, which more or less fits properly his sizeable, grown-man's body, only his right hand, St Stephen's right hand is seen in the picture holding up the count's left upper thigh, the left one, the left hand, as indicated by his left arm, which is shown going down, doing the same to the count's right one and is consequently hidden by it, the hand, the right hand of St Stephen is tiny, disproportionally small even for his teenager's body, this almost definitely also for compositional reasons, to counteract properly the left hand of the first knight of Santiago that fills the void, the big empty black space above the count's slumping body on top and between the two saints on the sides, like an open white rose, to which, that is, to the left hand of the first knight of Santiago, it, St Stephen's right hand is intended to be a companion, as it is open in the opposite direction, the two hands therefore seeming to be holding up the lower body of the count together, as is well known, the archbishop of Toledo, Gaspar de Quiroga y Vela, is depicted as St Augustin, I have not seen any indication who might be the model for St Stephen, but I have to say once again that I am certain that every figure in the painting, at least in the terrestrial part of the painting, must be an image of someone real, and so, the figure of St Stephen must be a portrait of a person, of some youth, El Greco knew and valued or admired, he, St Stephen is frequently referred to as the protomartyr, in other words, the first martyr, the first martyr of Christianity, and is typically depicted as a young man, he is said to have been a Hellenistic, or a Greek-speaking, Jew, who was a deacon of a church in Jerusalem, who angered Jewish religious authorities with his preaching and as a result was stoned to death, the stoning is depicted in the picture in an image at the bottom of the right side of the saint's robe, he is down on his knees, his head thrown back, his eyes raised to heaven, with two naked male figures holding big stones in their raised

hands above him, ready to hurl them down, one further
away, with a small stone in his likewise raised right hand,
and one next to the latter, on his left, bending down to pick
up another big stone, so as to hurl it, what a way to go! I
came back to the apartment a year later, in the summer, for
summer vacation, so to speak, some vacation, the place
empty, empty of people, of life, not of furniture, not yet, that
is, the stretch of the sea sticking up above the roof of the big
café seen through the door in my study and the window in
the living/dining room a cemetery, a vast treeless cemetery
full of the boring, identical liquid tombstones of the waves,
came in the sleeping car from Madrid, not to lie down next
to a wife as to a soft, warm mirror, but next to a mirror like a
hard, cold wife, no, no, wrong, forgot, not in a sleeping car,
not in a train from Madrid either, but by boat from England,
was pretty choppy at night, remember, nearly got sick, yes,
so, came by boat from England, was desperately searching
for someone, searching over half of the surface of the globe,
stayed with some friends in London for a week, I think, a
woman I had a crush on once, an unreciprocated crush, and
her husband, their live-in South African, white South African
nanny, who took care of their daughter, as I found out years

later from the woman and her husband, had a crush on ME, was disappointed, pissed, I didn't visit her at night in her room, which was next to mine, I was pissed, disappointed myself when I found out too, she was young and not bad-looking, would have liked to bed her, but didn't want to offend my hosts, too late, anyway, so, alone in the apartment, I realized, I couldn't keep it, couldn't keep coming back to it, had to sell it, put out the feelers through my friend Antonio, the man who built the place, the apartment building, lived on the top, the seventh floor above, within a day or two had a buyer, she was a woman, I mean it was a couple, a married couple with no children, she came alone, wore the pants, I mean, wore a dress or a skirt, but wore the pants in the family, looked like she wore the pants in the family even when she had nothing on, probably especially when she had nothing on, she walked around confidently, resolutely, inspecting the rooms, kitchen, bathrooms, first once, then again and again, I began to be turned on, she looked good, Spanish women in my opinion rarely do, look like horses, bony and with those long narrow faces, faces like men's, Spanish men can be attractive with their strong, masculine features, but women no, look too much like the men, like

215

men in drag, in all the years I lived there, I didn't see more than a handful of beautiful feminine women, German women too, rarely attractive, boney, the most attractive, Italian and Slavic, especially Slavic, with those soft feminine features and grey, blue or gray, but especially gray, pearl-gray, Slavic eyes, Slavic women, yes, very feminine and very attractive, anyway, she, the buyer woman, actually looked nice, not beautiful, but attractive, Italian perhaps, so here we are going through the apartment, just me and her, and all of a sudden I started thinking about *Last Tango in Paris*, the movie, Bertolucci's movie *Last Tango in Paris* with Marlon Brando and Maria Schneider, in which he buggers her as she is looking over the apartment, I think, she wants to buy or rent from him, I used to think of myself as looking like Brando when I was young, so, so what? so here I am an older Brando, so I begin to get the same idea myself, except not to bugger, but to do it the normal way, and not standing up, but on a bed, after all, there were three nice ones available, I must have shown it because she showed no interest in me at the beginning, but then, at one point, began to throw me flashing, dangerous looks, my God, I thought, she's willing, ready, but I chickened out in the end, didn't want any trouble, had had enough of them recently, that was probably part of the reason I didn't go after that chick in London, anyway, and she'll probably ask for a discount on the apartment, I reasoned, so I held back, began to ignore her, in the end, she agreed, said she'd buy the place at the price I was asking, but said, she'd have to come over with her husband, he had to agree too, the normal thing, add mere formality, but it was clear the decision they'd buy the place was final, so the next day they came both, he, a pudgy little accountant, but was apparently bringing in the money, felt pity for him, was glad nothing happened between me and his wife, would have felt guilty for putting horns on him, on his miserable little head, but she again gave me a few of those dangerous flashy looks as we were going through the apartment, which I ignored, didn't understand it, what for? she knew I was leaving, probably just to tease me, to exercise her inborn female seductive skills, anyway, so, he agreed, of course, and I sold the apartment, was going to ship over the furniture back home, don't know what for, as I had a houseful of it at home already, there was nowhere to put it, probably would have tried to sell it there, but completely by chance ran into an American couple, from

Yuriy Tarnawsky

Seattle, I think, actually, a family, husband, wife, and two sons, one son, college-age, as I recall, and the other a teenager, who were looking for furniture, and they bought it off me, I was asking exactly the same I got it for, they were suspicious, had them check with the maker, he corroborated, and they bought the things, they paid me with a check, which actually was honored, worked out alright, it was a substantial sum, was the nest egg, the seed from which grew my ultimate pitiful count's estate, they, the couple, were to make the arrangements to ship the things home after I left, all through Antonio, all to go through Antonio, the money for the apartment too, which I got a few months later, courtesy of him, it was nearly impossible to get money out of Spain in those days, taxes, and restrictions, and all, he sent it to his business friend in Mexico and the guy got it over to me, no taxes, no hassle, all kosher, legal, somehow, great! he was a great friend, Tere, his wife Tere, Teresa, and sister Jose, Jóse, not José, for Josefina, took care of the rest, of the other things like dishes, rugs, table cloths, and so on, they bought a couple of trunks, packed everything, and shipped them via boat, everything came alright, undamaged, except one big beautiful deep serving dish from Talavera crushed, crushed like something inside me.

28

ST AUGUSTIN, I mean, Gaspar de Quiroga y Vela, who is generally considered to be the figure that stands in for St Augustin in the painting, lived from 1512 to 1594 and at the time El Greco worked on it was the General Inquisitor of Spain and the Archbishop of Toledo, which made him the Primate of the Spanish Church or one of the most important religious figures in the country, and a cardinal to boot, he was born in a small town in the province of Ávila with a wonderfully poetic name of Madrigal de las Altas Torres, meaning Madrigal of the Tall Towers, and was educated, of course, at, where else, if not at the University of Salamanca, obtaining from it a degree of Doctor of Law and Theology, he is said to have been a patron of El Greco, now, it was in 1577, the year that he came to Spain from Italy, that El Greco did that big painting *El Espolio* for the Toledo cathedral and it was also in 1577 that Gaspar de Quiroga y Vela was named the Archbishop of Toledo, so it would be natural to assume that the friendship between the two stems from that time, that is, from Gaspar de Quiroga y Vela commissioning the painting and being pleased with El Greco's work, but it turns out not to be so, as the commission was actually granted by the dean of the Toledo cathedral Diego de Castilla through the intervention of his son Louis, whom El Greco befriended in Rome, it is possible therefore, that Gaspar de Quiroga y Vela, being new to the cathedral, decided to rely on Diego de Castilla's good judgement and not to get involved in the contract negotiations, or, which is more likely, that he was named archbishop after the commission was granted, at any rate, he must have liked El Greco's work and felt compelled to support him, so, it would make sense that El Greco, astute businessman that he was, would have Gaspar de Quiroga y Vela in the painting and would allocate to him one of the most important spots in it, since this is so, it seems extremely unlikely that whoever is the model for the figure of St Stephen in the painting is a person of little importance, who is there only because El Greco liked him, no, El Greco, once again, was too astute a businessman to do that, to pass up the opportunity of advancing his interests by wasting such an important spot in the painting on someone who would do nothing for him, a spot in its very center, facing one of the most important religious figures in the country, and situated over the body of the count so that the image of the person in the spot would be reflected in the count's armor, no! the youth, the young man who stands in for the saint, for St Stephen, then, must be a person of pretty high importance, almost certainly not directly, because of his age, but through his relation to someone else, someone older than he, who is important, his father, or uncle, or someone like that, it is strange therefore that there seems to be no mention anywhere of who he might be, strange? no, why am I saying that? El Greco didn't advertise anywhere who the people he painted were, after all, we don't know for instance that the figure of St Augustin is Gaspar de Quiroga y Vela, people are guessing it is because of its resemblance to extant portraits of the Archbishop, we don't know that the first knight of Santiago, the man, who makes that eloquent two-hand gesture, is the mayor of Toledo, that there is Antonio de Covarrubias and his brother Diego in the painting, that the two priests are Pedro Ruiz Durón and Andrés Núñez de Madrid, and so on, and so forth, we don't even know that the eighth figure in the row of stokers is El Greco himself, these are all educated guesses, that's all, and they all could be wrong, but the youth who stands in for St Stephen was too young to have had portraits of himself painted so that we could compare his image to another one, and so nobody has taken a chance to guess who he might be, and he is probably there because his father or uncle or some other relative was important, that's all, and that could have been anybody, anybody in the picture or anybody at all,   although that possibility seems less likely since El Greco packed his painting with the cream of the crop of the *hidalguía* of Spain, of Castile, so why would he put in the picture an important man's son but not the man himself? it doesn't make sense, no, he, the youth, the image of St Stephen, could be, for instance, the son, the illegitimate son of Quiroga, of the Archbishop, why not? it's quite possible, Popes had illegitimate children, if I'm not mistaken, can't remember right now who, a Borgia perhaps, but there were some, one at least for sure, and the society didn't frown on it so much then, not as much as now, I mean later, for a while later, look at El Greco himself, his son Jorge Manuel, whose mother he never married, and that apparently applied to clergy too, yes, the Archbishop Gaspar de Quiroga y Vela seems a good candidate for being St Stephen's, the youth's who's standing in for St Stephen, farther in the painting, makes sense, the two of them, father and son, holding up the body of the count together, yes! and there is Jorge Manuel, El Greco's illegitimate son, right there, next to the saint, to the youth, pointing his finger at him as if saying, he's like me, he's illegitimate too, and, God! I've just noticed, there's El Greco himself right above him, his hand over the youth's head, yes, very likely, very, very likely, that he, the youth standing in for St Stephen, is the Archbishop's illegitimate son, and speaking of illegitimate sons, the other day, no, not the other day, yesterday, actually yesterday, I was in the cathedral, trying to get some scoop on the Archbishop, on Gaspar de Quiroga y Vela, some scoop, not to see if I would find proof of his having had an illegitimate son, as if there was any chance there could be one there, because I wasn't thinking of that yesterday, got the idea just now, so not to get a scoop, but to look at his, at the Archbishop's portrait by Luis de Velasco that hangs in the *Sala Capitular,* in the Capitulary Room, to compare it to El Greco's portrait, as if that would change anything, as if I'd prove by this one way or another if he was the model for the saint, for St Augustin, after all those experts have already decided that he was, so who am I to argue with them? anyway, I was there, in the Capitulary Room, not to get any scoop, but out of curiosity, to have a look at the other portrait and compare it to the painting, well, it wasn't easy with all those portraits hanging in a row on the wall, all looking the same, it wasn't easy, but I finally did it, I found it, this one, I mean that one, the one by Velasco, didn't look very much like the one by El Greco at all, a miter and a robe, yes, an old man, yes, a beard, yes, but Velasco's shorter and well-trimmed, compared to El Greco's long and exuberant one, Velasco's portrait was painted in 1595, however, potentially close to ten years later, so the man could have changed, could have had his beard trimmed, and El Greco's, El Greco's beard almost certainly was compositionally motivated, to give the saint, St Augustin more stature and go with his super exuberant robe, anyway, they didn't pay that much attention to similarity in those days, general features and the aura, that's all, and that applies to El Greco too, as for example in the two different portraits of Antonio de Covarrubias, the one in the painting, in the *Entierro,* and the other individual one, done just a few years later, in 1600, that hangs in the Prado, similar, as they say, but different, anyway, so, the conclusion was, similar but different, so what, Gaspar de Quiroga y Vela stays St Augustin and that's it, but the expedition, the whole endeavor, did lead to something, to an amorous, that is, to a near-amorous encounter, there was a woman, a young woman going through the hall, the Sala Capitular with me, one of three or four or perhaps five other figures who like the two of us were slinking along the walls, searching for something, frustrated at not being able to find the damned thing, since she was right next to me, I asked her if she knew where the portrait of the Archbishop was, she looked at me, startled, as if I'd done something threatening, but after composing herself said that she had no idea, it was her first time there, and moved on, walking quickly away from me, I kept following her, because I'd been moving in the same direction, and after a while, surprisingly, she began throwing me flashing, dangerous looks, quite a few of them, too, one after the other, my God, I thought, she thinks I made a pass at her and she's interested, willing, me? at my age? the way I feel and look? no way! yes way, there was no doubt that she was, but I didn't know how far it'd go, perhaps not far, judging by the way she reacted to my asking the question, possibly not far, anyway, that doesn't matter, and then I remembered my apartment, the selling of my apartment, the woman I wanted to screw and who wanted to be screwed by me, and I looked at her, at the woman in the hall, the Sala, saw her for the first time the way she was, and I nearly puked, my God! no wonder she's interested in me, a dog, a pack of dogs, not just one, no, not a pack, one's enough, just one skinny, skin-and-bones dog, dressed in black, all in black, short quilted black coat, short, too short black skirt, black tights, black flat men's boots, legs thin, really thin, almost like a spider's in those black tights, and she moved clumsily on them just like a spider, a black widow, screwing? screwing that? getting between those legs? having a son, an illegitimate son with her? I almost puked and darted out of the Sala, the cathedral, to make sure I wouldn't have a chance to do that, that I'd be as far away from her as possible, I stayed in touch with Antonio over many years, we wrote each other regularly, he was a funny guy, rich, they had a number of apartments and apartment houses, but he'd send his letter by boat, it took weeks, sometimes a month or more for one of them to get to me, I hinted at the problem, but he never responded, never changed, rich people can be like that, stingy and generous at the same time, eventually they broke up, Tere left him, three kids, Tonio, Jaime, and Pilar, and she left him, Spain was changing, becoming modern, women were emancipated, felt they deserved, no, had an obligation to be happy, at one point the letters stopped coming, I wrote once, twice, then Tonio, the oldest son, wrote me, *Tengo noticias más tristes posible para ti*, the saddest news possible, he'd died, Antonio had died, of lung cancer, I think, he smoked a lot, I never set foot in that town again after getting rid of my place, why would I? you can't unend an end.

29

MY SON, I mean, El Greco's son Jorge Manuel is the first
figure in the third row down from the top, just one shy of the
second one, that is, of the last of them all, of Don Gonzalo
Ruiz de Toledo, the Count of Orgaz, he, Jorge Manuel is
kneeling on his left knee, his right leg bent and extended
forward, his right arm reaching out back, its hand holding
awkwardly a flaming torch that is leaning away at the top, his
left arm raised and bent, the index finger pointing at
something that looks like an open white rose or, even more,
a lush, ripe, white peony embroidered on the lower part of
the wide sleeve of St Stephen's oversized robe, and at the
same time at the sagging body of the count, there is a
triangular edge of a white sheet of paper, or actually of a few
sheets of white paper folded together, sticking out of the
pocket of his black tunic that looks a bit like a girl's dress,
with some writing on it in Greek, ending in, what looks like,
El Greco's last name, **Theotokópoulos** broken up into two

lines, and four characters at the very end that apparently stand for 1578, the year Jorge Manuel was born, I think it was customary for a while in European countries to use letters instead of the Arabic symbols after adapting the decimal system, by this El Greco is acknowledging his fatherhood of the boy, whose mother **Jerónima de las Cuevas** he never married, and specifies the year of his birth, the painting was done between March of 1586 and early 1588, so the boy would have been between eight and nine years old when his father painted him, he, Jorge Manuel, became a painter himself, working in his father's studio, never achieving much success, however, devoid of the extraordinary talents of his genial progenitor, even the copies of some of his father's works that he did, such as *El Espolio, Martyrdom of St Maurice*, and *St Martin and the Beggar*, which at first glance appear to be El Greco's, soon begin to shed their effect and make the viewer feel uncomfortable, something is not quite right in them, something appears to have gone askew, there is an original painting of his called *The Family of El Greco,* painted in 1605, when he was twenty-seven years old, which painfully reveals the limited scope of his talent, done almost in monochrome, in soft shades of charcoal-gray and brown with occasional dabs of white and reminiscent of Van Gogh's early painting *Potato Eaters*, it shows six figures, going from left to right, a cat, a young woman spinning, another one embroidering, an old woman with glasses on her nose looking on, and still another young woman standing up and leaning forward, her left hand steadying a toddler, perhaps two years old, clothed in what looks like a girl's dress, appearing however to be a boy, by family, Jorge Manuel must be referring to his mother's side, since El Greco came to Spain alone and was joined by his older brother Manoússos, by then an old man, only in 1603, when Jorge Manuel was twenty-five years old, this seems to be a recollection, or rather a reconstruction, from Jorge Manuel's infancy, the family cat, his two aunts, grandmother, mother, and himself, the figures are done crudely, with little detail, in particular the hands, most of which resemble a bear's frightening claws, each finger separate from its neighbor or neighbors, the precious space around them wasted, looking like ugly gaps in a person's mouth after extractions of teeth, compare the twenty-six figures in the row of stokers in his father's painting, each expertly interlinked with its surroundings like orthodontically perfectly formed and spaced teeth in a person's mouth, it is true that the figures in Van Gogh's painting also don't touch, but they are arranged in an interesting way rather than in a boring row and their gnarled shapes are replicated in the bodies of the others like reflections on the surface of rippling water, if anyone were inclined to dispute such valuation of the painting, let him or her examine the picture of the cat, it is sitting high up on a table, far removed from the people, contrary to its natural propensity for contact with other living creature for the sharing of warmth, it is oddly shaped, with a rigid body and a triangular head, looking like a stylized ceramic figurine rather than a live cat, Jorge Manuel was married twice, apparently becoming once a widower, and in 1614, after his father's death, turned to architecture, participating in the construction of the Toledo City Hall, the *Casa Consistorial*, the *Ayuntamiento,* in 1625 he became the master builder, sculptor, and architect of the Toledo cathedral, toward the end of his life was sued by Toledo's Hospital de Tavera for incompletion of the work contracted by his late father, lost the suit, was dispossessed of all his property, and died in penury in 1631, a son, a son devoid of talent, well, not quite devoid of talent, did have some talent, some artistic talent, probably more than an average person, but devoid of genius, of artistic genius, for sure, nowhere close to his father, but so what? a son, a son! El Greco loved him, was proud of him, and painting apparently wasn't his forte, I mean, his field, what he would have most liked to do, what he craved to do, after all, eventually he turned to architecture, it looks like he wasn't exceptional in it either, but how many architects in his time were? in all times in Spain, Herrera is the only name, the only figure whose name, as far as I know, we remember today, Jorge Manuel was said to have worked as architect in the *herrerian* style, as was everyone else at the time, a son, anyway, a son? did I have a son? as far as I know, no, not with the woman I was married to, barren, barren like a sunbaked field, a field of rock-hard, sunbaked clay, like a sunbaked concrete apron in front of a Southern California development garage, but outside? maybe outside of marriage? an illegitimate one or two? perhaps, but as far as I know, no, not likely, there were some abortions, at least one for sure, broke up with the woman right away after that, murdering your own child, ghastly, monstrous, she'd just started on a new career and didn't want to spoil it, to put a stick between the spokes of its wheel, a week of wavering, of arguing and screaming, and she was gone, good riddance! it wouldn't have worked anyway, would have been hell, she had two kids already, but maybe with someone else, it could be, it's possible, wouldn't it be wonderful if one day a young man, a handsome young man appeared in my doorway and said, Hi, dad, how are you? Been looking for you all my life and finally I've found you! It's so great, so great! or maybe he'd say, Where have you been all this time, you bastard, you old fucking bastard?! Why weren't you there? Why weren't you with me as I was growing up, when I need you most? no, he wouldn't be saying that, why would he have looked for me? to do something to me? to heap insults on me? to beat me up? to kill me? no, you don't build up hatred like that for someone you've never seen, no, no way, anyway, regardless, what would he do to me lying there in bed, half-dead, my head turned in his direction? I'd welcome him, tell him to step up, tell him I loved him, I didn't know he existed, would have adopted him, married his mother, if I'd known, would have taken care of him, nurtured him, helped him become himself, I'd kiss his still full, not yet bony cheeks, his shiny eyes, the slightly puffy eyelids, the thick dark eyebrows, the wavy chestnut hair, ask him to step back, so I'd have a better look at him, admire him, his slender, wiry frame, his figure gleaming with masculinity like a shiny ball bearing, me, myself, as I sat at the table I'd set outside and drank Portuguese rosé the day I moved into the first house I had bought, anyway, next time, next time or if I were starting over, no art, no fucking farty art, kids, children, lots and lots of children! no, not that many, two or three or four, of either gender, but preferably one of one and two of the other, doesn't matter how many of which, either is fine, imagine what it'd be like if I had three children, and those had three each, and the children of my children, that is my grandchildren, also had three each, which would be my great grandchildren, which at my age, assuming each generation was between twenty-five and thirty years apart, then if I were lying on my deathbed in my count's manor house or palace and not in my shabby rented room here in Toledo, and all those offspring of mine were gathered around me, there'd be, let's see how many, three plus, three times three, which is nine, plus three times nine, which is twenty-seven, so, there'd be three, plus nine, plus twenty seven or thirty-nine people, thirty-nine persons with my genes in them, copies of me, partial copies but still copies, seeing me off on my final journey, but staying behind to carry me into the future, my God, thirty-nine! and that's the minimum! it's conceivable that the generations were shorter, in some cases at least shorter, twenty-two/twenty-three years, so that at my age I could have great-great grandchildren, of whom there'd potentially be twenty-seven times three or eighty-one! eighty-one additional offspring! adding eighty-one to thirty-nine gives one hundred twenty, so I could have one hundred twenty of my offspring gathered around me as I lay dying, this is more than, actually more than four times the number of the persons who are attending Don Gonzalo Ruiz de Toledo's reburial, the figure is one hundred twenty divided by twenty-nine rather than thirty, but I can't figure it out now, so, one hundred twenty! one hundred twenty persons, it'd fill the whole *Casa Consistorial*, the *Ayuntamiento,* the City Hall, that is, not just the boiler room in its basement, probably the whole damn building, the whole damn building! this isn't dying, it's leaving and staying behind, it's going to heaven and remaining on earth, it's being immortal, it's great!

30

DON GONZALO RUIZ de Toledo was a native of Toledo, lived from around 1256 to 1323, was among other things the IV Señor, or Lord, of Orgaz, the chief notary of Castile, the majordomo of king Alfonso XI, and mayor of Toledo, descended from the illustrious Toledan families of the Toledo and the Illán and through the latter was related to Pedro Paleólogo, the third son of the emperor of Byzantium, but the fact that he was of Greek origin doesn't seem to have had any relation to El Greco's doing the painting, there is no mention of El Greco's anywhere referring to the fact even though he was fiercely loyal to his ethnic background and pointed it out wherever he could, the family, the Ruiz family, was elevated to the title of *Conde* or Count by king Carlos I in 1520, through which act he, don Gonzalo, was entitled to be called count at the time El Greco did the painting, he must have been sixty-seven when he died, but in the picture looks as if he were in his thirties or at the most early forties, some sources give 1260 as the year of his birth, which would make him sixty-three at the time of his death, but that wouldn't have any, or at least much impact on his appearance, his face is youthful, without a trace of a wrinkle, and there isn't the trace of a single *cana,* a gray hair, in his head of tick black hair and full beard, but of course, El Greco wasn't trying to be realistic in the painting, his aim was to produce an effective image, an image which would leave a moving impression on the viewer, and seeing a vigorous young man being lowered into a grave is more sad than seeing an old grizzled one, and yes, of course, let us not forget that what we are witnessing in the picture is not the count's burial, but his reburial, which was in 1327, or four years after his death, you can imagine what we would be seeing if El Greco had tried to be even remotely true to reality, I suspect that hardly anything would have been staying together and the two saints would have had literally a mess on their hands, a coffin surely must have been used, otherwise the picture would have been scaring away anyone who took a glance at it and the chapel, sometimes filled to capacity these days, filled with tourists, that is, not with pious Toledans, of whom, I suspect, there aren't many, would be empty most of the time, how the two poor saints dealt with the task is another story, but, the chance they were involved in it, let's face it, is not very high, it is in fact very close to, that is, practically equal to nil, but that's still another story, anyway, in the picture we have, the saints are holding up the body of the count, St Stephen, the legs, on the left, and St Augustin, the back and shoulders, on the right, well, holding up is not quite the word, I mean, the words, St Stephen's small, child's right hand with its fingers pressed together is under the count's left thigh, but inches away from it, gently touching the fold of a white shroud which isn't flattened by the thigh's weight, St Augustin's hands are not seen, although he stands in the correct position to be holding up the body, it, the body sags over a white shroud, which hangs loose, without showing any effect of the weight of the body over it, once more, an indication of El Greco's paying attention to the laws of art rather than to those of nature, the composition, it is generally admitted, has been suggested by Titian's *The Entombment of Christ,* done around 1520, a painter whom El Greco admired, unlike Michelangelo, who, he claimed, didn't know how paint, in the Titian painting, the body, Christ's body is nude, with the left arm hanging down and the right one held up high by a man who's helping out with the burial, in El Greco's, on the other hand, the count is wearing a shiny black suit of armor, decorated all over with golden designs, his hands are piously crossed on his belly, the left thigh, the one St Stephen is supposedly holding up, reflects the white shroud below it, there are reflections of the surroundings, that is, of the vestments of the two saints, all over the suit of armor, golden and red, augmenting and enhancing the designs, one stands out in particular, a vague golden-red stain on the left side of the count's chest, right over his heart, that is hard to describe, but could be the outline of a human figure, and must be that of the facing saint, in other words, of St Stephen, the count's eyes and mouth are closed, the expression on his face serene, he seems to be resting or sleeping, rather than dead, feeling safe to be finding himself, both literally and figuratively speaking, in good hands, I don't know if there are any extant portraits of Don Gonzalo, I haven't seen any references to one, but even if there were, that is, if one exists, it is very unlikely that what we have in the painting is El Greco's copy of it, after all, he didn't reproduce the pictures of the two saints from existing paintings, but used his own models, the face of Don

Gonzalo, then, must be, or almost definitely is a portrait of some other person, a person of high, of very high stature, I've seen no references to this, no suggestions, which is strange, but I feel that on this issue I stand on firm ground and that the image of Don Gonzalo is that of some important figure of the Spanish *hidalguía* of the times of El Greco, this brings up once again the issue of who is the prototype of St Stephen, I've suggested that he may be the illegitimate son of Archbishop Gaspar de Quiroga y Vela, but this isn't certain, it is a hypothesis, a pretty good hypothesis, but nothing more, but the figure of St Stephen is reflected in the heart of the count, does it mean then that he, St Stephen, is related to the prototype, to the prototype of the count? could they be respectively son and father? I think, they could, but this is just another hypothesis which is impossible to prove, and we will never know the answer to the question and must leave the subject alone, another issue is the death of the count, I've seen it being referred to as murder and as a saint's, which to me suggests a martyr's, but the vast majority of mentions say simply death or he died, which implies natural death, dying of natural causes, most likely of old age rather than of a disease, this to me is incongruous, something must be wrong here, it isn't possible that Don Gonzalo died a violent death and people would be calling it simply death just out of laziness, not bothering to go into the details, no, definitely not, so, I think that he, Don Gonzalo, died of natural causes, let's call it of old age, which at sixty-seven at that time could have safely been called that, and I feel I may know the origin of the murder theory, in my persistent search for the explanation, I have come to only one ancient source which seems to have a bearing on this issue, there is a play by Guillén de Castro y Belvis published in 1618, based on old *Romanceros,* called *Mocedades de Cid,* that is, *Youthful Years of Cid*, dealing with the Spanish hero Rodrigo Díaz de Vivar, known as El Cid, who liberated Spain from the Moors, he, El Cid, was married to a woman named Jimena Díaz, whose father bore the title of Conde de Orgaz, so, according to the play, prior to marrying Jimena, El Cid kills her father, while defending his own father from the assault by the former, in Act II of the play, there is an exchange of words between the King and one Peransules, in which the latter, answering the former's question, who killed the Count of Orgaz, says, *Un rapaz ha muerto al Conde de Orgaz,* A predator has killed the Count of Orgaz, there you are! there you have it! this must be it, the source of the confusion, whoever thought that Don Gonzalo Ruiz de Toledo was murdered must have heard of or read this and thought he learned a fact, but he was wrong, he had the wrong count in mind, and as to saintly death meaning martyrdom, that may be simply explained by the linguistic phenomenon of polysemy, that is, a saintly death may be the death of someone who died as a martyr and was declared a saint partly because of how he died, or of one who led the life of a saint and who died a peaceful death, but anyway, how do we, how do all of us ultimately do it? die? not that I am an expert on this, not a trace of experience so far, but let me count the ways as best I can, the best, the easiest, is to do it shortly after you're born of something without pain, before you're aware of yourself, before you understand the concepts of to be and not to be, no anticipation, no fear, no trembling, you didn't know you were and won't know you're not, and on top of it, no pain, easy come, easy go, or perhaps, not so easy come, but easy go, next, all sorts of unexpected quick events, that's the key, unexpected and quick, it's the waiting, the awareness that it's coming that is the painful, frightening thing, and then, if it goes on and on, it's a real drag, real pain, especially if it hurts, if it hurts really badly, if its short, a second or two, or less than a second, who cares? you can take anything for less than a second, like a microsecond, you won't even know it was there, so, unexpected and short, you're walking down the street and a stray bullet hits you in the head, or someone comes up from behind and fires into the base of your skull, you're lucky! it's great! he did you a big favor!! perhaps a loud noise and the onset of a great flood of light, of still just white light like dawn breaking outside the window, no pain, no trace of pain yet, and it's gone, everything's gone, you never were and you're not, wonderful! great! a head-on crash in a car, not so good, better than some ways, but not as good as a bullet in the brain, a loud bang, the sound of rubber screeching, metal crunching, glass cracking and turning milky, opaque, the onset of pain in the chest, forehead, nose, hands, knees, whatever, not so good, probably lasting seconds, enough time to conclude, I'm going, not that good, no, but better than lying under a pile of bricks for hours or days and knowing how it'll end, oh, yes, a bullet, a rifle bullet in the heart or forehead with your hands tied behind your back not so good either, not much pain, but expectation, lots and lots of expectation, ditto for the guillotine blade coming down on the back of your neck, could be months or years of waiting, expectation, no good, bad, terrible! a bomb or a mine, a bomb from above and a mine from below, not certain, if powerful, if instantaneous, then great, of course, everything instantaneous, no expectation, anticipation, that's great, but if partial and then waiting, very bad, terrible, pain and anticipation, drawn-out anticipation and drawn out pain, terrible, like an illness, horrible, so everything short and, especially, not anticipated, great, not one and/or the other, then bad, horrible if both, so illness, bad, especially if prolonged, bad, pain and anticipation, but at the very end probably not so bad, weakened and tired, sick of it, of the illness, the treatment, so it coming as a salvation, relief, a yearned-for relief, thank God, it finally came, old age probably similar, Don Gonzalo, oh, yes, I forgot, he died on December 9, December 3 old style, the fiesta of Santa Leocadia, the patron saint of Toledo, when I thought he, the count had been murdered, murdered by a predator, a *rapaz*, murdered on the fiesta day of the patron saint of Toledo, having read those two lines out of context, *Un rapaz ha muerto al Conde de Orgaz,* since he was the mayor of the city, I imagined it having happened as he was walking through the crowds, perhaps shaking hands, although I'm not sure they shook hands then, probably not, anyway, so, I imagined him, Don Gonzalo pushing his way through the crowd, justled on all sides, and the fiend, the murderer, stuck a knife in his chest or back or side, a political murder, a rivalry, or personal revenge, whatever the motive may have been, that could have been not so bad, depending on the place, I mean, where the knife entered, if straight in the heart, then not too bad, not as fast as a bullet, but pretty quick, not too much pain, in the back or side, the belly, could have been not too much pain, and then the weakening, not giving a damn, followed by nothing, by peace, relief, good, fine, but if not, if pain and waiting, then not so good, but that didn't happen, of course, old age, old age, that might be not too bad sometimes, depending on what part of old age you go from, if a prolonged illness, then as was said, bad, but if just fatigue, deterioration, then not so bad, potentially quite good in fact, one of the best, potentially the best, awareness, yes, but you're not hurting, you're tired, you've done all you wanted, all you had to do, you've carried out your duties, you're surrounded by your loved ones, everyone's fine, OK, so you can go, then yes, then very good, then actually the best, the job finished, well done, the house left in order.

Checklist of Previous JEF Titles